Paper
Chains

Also by Elaine Vickers

Like Magic

Paper Chains

Elaine Vickers

HARPER
An Imprint of HarperCollinsPublishers

www.harpercollinschildrens.com

Library of Congress Control Number: 2017938988

ISBN 978-0-06-241434-2 (trade bdg.)

Typography by Abby Dening

Illustration by Sara Not

17 18 19 20 21   PC/LSCH   10 9 8 7 6 5 4 3 2 1

First Edition

for my family

Katie

Chapter 1

EVERY STORY HAS *a beginning.*

That's what Katie's teacher kept saying all week, and even though Katie had just been set free for five days of Thanksgiving break, those words echoed through her ears. They taunted her as she made her way across the playground and down the sidewalk; they haunted her as she listened to the buzz of voices around her.

Of course, her teacher hadn't been trying to freak anybody out. She'd been talking about pilgrims and the Wampanoag and Plymouth, Massachusetts, where they'd be going on a field trip in the spring. "History!" Ms. Decker had said. "You have to know your history. Every story has a beginning, and you can't move forward in the right direction unless you know where you've been."

Farther down the crumbly brick sidewalk, Katie spotted a hockey jacket that had to belong to her best friend, Ana. And in that very instant, Ana turned and spotted Katie too. It had been like that for them since the first day they'd met—saying things and doing things at just the same time, even though they were so different.

"Hey," said Ana, pulling her hair into a lumpy, loopy black ponytail. Katie touched the fancy braid her mom had fixed for her that morning, still so tight it pulled at her skin.

"Sorry I didn't wait," Ana said. "Mikey just took off." Ana's little brother waited for them at the end of the block, studying something in his red-mittened hands.

"I don't think we can come over today," Ana said, lowering her voice. "But watch for my signal over the break. Maybe even tonight, once it's dark. I'm feeling like we might need some adventure this Thanksgiving!" Ana wiggled her eyebrows and smiled her up-to-something smile. Then she hurried down the sidewalk to catch up to Mikey before he crossed the street alone.

Katie blew on her fingers to warm them up. Was she ready for an Ana-size adventure?

It had been four months since Katie and her parents had moved to Boston. The summer had been blisteringly hot and achingly lonely, but fall had been much better. As soon as school had started and Ana had noticed there was another fifth-grade girl in the neighborhood, she'd made an announcement.

"You and me, Goldilocks," she'd said, nodding at Katie's long, honey-colored hair. "We're best friends now."

Normal kids couldn't announce friendships and hand out nicknames, just like that, but Ana was definitely not normal.

In a good way.

Mostly.

Katie and Ana lived just one street apart, and those streets curved so that their backyards faced the same small pond. At Katie's house, Ana had quickly gone from ringing the doorbell and waiting like regular visitors to knocking-then-walking to coming right through the kitchen door.

"It just makes more sense," she'd told Katie. "That way I can grab a snack on my way to find you, and I'll still get there faster."

"I guess you're more like Goldilocks now," Katie had teased her.

But Ana had disagreed. "Goldilocks was an intruder," she'd explained. "I'm like family."

Katie loved that Ana felt so comfortable at her house, but she didn't agree about the "like family" part. Family was a quilt—safe and familiar, patched together maybe, and sometimes wrapped a little too tight. Ana was more like a superhero cape, always off on adventures, flapping whichever way the wind blew.

Now the wind nudged Katie along as she hurried up the path to her brand-new, hundred-year-old house. White siding, black shutters, and a bright red door, all perfectly symmetrical. It was nothing like her Salt Lake house with its big backyard and gray stone that matched the mountains. Her Boston house couldn't match the mountains because there were no mountains here, and Katie missed them more than she ever would have guessed. How were you supposed to know which way was east without mountains, unless the sun was rising? People here acted like the Charles River or Boston Harbor should be a clue, but how was that supposed to work when you couldn't always see them?

Katie reached for the knob, but before her fingers touched the cold metal, the door swung open. Suddenly, the world was warm and smelled like gingerbread as Katie's mom folded her into her arms.

"My girl!" she said. "Home with me for five whole days. That's what I'm thankful for."

Katie and her mom walked to the kitchen, where a thick square of gingerbread and a tall glass of milk already waited on the counter. Katie's mom tucked a short, kitten-gray curl behind her ear and perched her reading glasses on the end of her nose.

"Eat up; then you can tell me about your day while I finish these pie crusts. And you'd better start from the beginning."

There it was again.

Every story has a beginning.

In spite of the warmth of the well-worn kitchen, Katie shivered. Her story had a beginning too, of course. The trouble was that nobody knew what it was. Or nobody on this side of the ocean, anyway. Katie's story only seemed to stretch back as far as one closeup picture of her two-year-old self, looking sad and lonely in an orphanage. Or maybe it only stretched back to her very first, fuzzy memory: cold air on a hot day, blowing like magic from two gray rectangles inside a shiny silver car.

According to Katie's parents, this had happened when she was three years old. They said she'd been so mesmerized by the air conditioner the first time she'd felt it—letting the air flow between her fingers, puff into her mouth, whisper in her ears—that they'd sat with her in the driveway for almost an hour that day.

The day they'd brought her home.

"Okay, forget the beginning," said her mom, smiling. "Just tell me something!"

So Katie told her mom about the other parts of her day. It was easy to talk about *now* and *today* and even *tomorrow*. Ms. Decker's *history* was the hard part. When she'd talked about beginnings, Katie had wanted to raise her hand and ask, "What if you don't know the beginning?" Not that Katie wanted to tell the whole class about her adoption. She definitely, definitely didn't. She hadn't even told Ana.

Katie and her parents talked about the adoption once in a while, but it always gave Katie a twisty sort of pinch inside, and she suspected her parents felt the same way. Katie never brought it up herself. She could never find the right words.

I wonder what it's like in Russia sounded too much like *I wish I were there instead.*

Do you think my birth mother has blond hair? sounded like *I'd rather be like her than like you.*

And *tell me about my birth parents* sounded like *tell me about my* real *parents.*

But she didn't mean that at all, and nobody knew anything about her birth parents anyway. Katie only had one lonely photo from her life before; it stared back at her from a small frame in the living room. Some days it didn't even feel like a picture of her. And other days, it felt like the *only* true picture of her. Katie didn't tell her parents about those days.

Katie's mom pinched the edges of a piecrust into perfectly even pleats. "When you're finished with your snack, do you think you could find the turkey platter and the cornucopia centerpiece for me? There should be a Thanksgiving box in the attic somewhere."

"Okay." Katie eyed the piecrusts. Piecrusts meant pie filling, and those were the bowls she liked to scrape clean. "Can I help with anything else?"

Katie's mom frowned at an imperfect piecrust pinch. "No, I think I'd better handle this. You took your medication today, didn't you?"

In the seven years since her surgery, Katie had never missed a day of medication. She tried to keep the exasperation out of her voice as she answered.

"Yes, Mom. I took my medication today."

"That's good." Her mom whirled the finished piecrust away and slid the next one toward her. "Up to the attic, please."

When Katie had climbed the two sets of narrow, creaky stairs and tugged the cord of the dangling bulb, she stopped to catch her breath and survey the attic. The first time she'd seen it, the space had felt almost spooky, with nothing but dark, angled corners and dusty floorboards. But now it was too packed to be scary, full of towers of boxes with labels like *Leftover Doodads* and *???* written by her dad in fat black Sharpie.

The attic was the reason their house stayed clean and presentable on the first two floors. If anything didn't have a perfect place or fit just so, it went upstairs. There were times when Katie felt more at home in the dim, drafty hodgepodge of the attic than anywhere else. Some of her summer projects were up here too—the suitcase she'd turned into a dollhouse, the chess set she'd made from a sanded-down tabletop and her mom's box of old knobs and buttons. Even the vintage typewriter she'd fixed up with her dad.

Katie wandered through the narrow, jumbled aisles between the boxes, searching for the word "Thanksgiving." But the creak of the floorboards and the taste of the air made the attic feel so old and so full of possibility that it gave Katie another idea too.

Every story has a beginning. Maybe somewhere in these boxes she could find out about hers.

Through the thick glass of the attic window, Katie saw snowflakes drifting down, soft white against the feather gray of the clouds. Snowflakes were nothing like the bellow of thunder or the urgent speed of rain. They didn't beg to be noticed, and as she watched each snowflake's small journey, guided by gravity and tiny breaths of wind, Katie felt like she was being told a secret.

Finally, she thought. It had been North-Pole cold all

November, but it hadn't snowed even once. Katie's dad had promised her the snow was coming soon, though—and plenty of it. It was hard to believe the season could change so completely—from miserable cold to magical *winter*—with something so small.

Katie let her gaze drift with the flakes until it fell upon an old box just under the window. The cardboard was soft and sagging, and the stripe of yellowing tape across the top looked like it had been sealing the box shut for years. Somehow that made Katie want to open it even more.

The box wasn't wide enough for the Thanksgiving platter or tall enough for the centerpiece, and it had no fat black Sharpie label at all. But it called to Katie just the same. She ripped back the tape and flipped the flaps open, telling herself not to be disappointed if it only held old vinyl records or scratchy sweaters.

Instead, the box was filled with things so beautiful and unexpected, they took Katie's breath away.

A pocket watch with delicate designs surrounding a bird, graceful but fierce.

A pair of carved candlesticks made of honey-colored wood.

A nutcracker, solid and strong in his soldier's uniform.

A smooth figurine painted like a round peasant woman that cracked in half to reveal another smaller figurine, and another, and another, and another, until finally Katie uncovered the smallest one, barely bigger than the tip of her pinkie. Nesting dolls, she thought they were called. Each one had the same curvy letters painted on the bottom—like initials, but in another language.

The things in the box weren't unusual—Katie had a watch sitting in her nightstand, and there were nutcrackers and candlesticks that they'd unpack from other attic boxes before the leftover turkey was all eaten.

But everything in this box seemed to be from another place and time, both familiar and unfamiliar all at once. They stirred a memory in her even fuzzier and farther away than the cool air in the silver car.

Katie picked up the things, one by one, and gathered

them in her lap, wondering who had made them, and how. Could she learn to carve like this if she practiced? To paint so perfectly? She fit the nesting dolls back together, each inside the one just bigger. *Inside her mother*, Katie thought. *They all fit right inside their mother. The way I fit inside my mother once.*

As she examined the remarkable pieces, Katie couldn't imagine they belonged to her parents. But the attic had been empty when they'd moved in.

So if they didn't belong to her parents, whose were they? Only one other person lived here. One other person with pieces of a past life that were still a mystery.

A knot in Katie's chest began to ease, and the drafts creeping in the cracks around the attic windows seemed to draw all the almost-magic to her. Then Katie knew the answer, and the falling snow seemed to whisper that she was right.

They're mine.

Katie

Chapter 2

THEY'RE MINE.

The words came so swift and strong to Katie's mind that she might have spoken them out loud. The strange, beautiful creations seemed to reach into her past and whisper the real beginning of her story. They felt so much a part of Katie that she didn't even want her parents to know she'd found them. She could visit the box whenever she wanted, and the beautiful things would belong only to her.

The thrill of her find, of her new secret, made Katie's heart beat a little faster. The heart inside her hadn't always been hers, so she had to pay extra attention to it, even with the medication. And even now, there was a flicker of worry that she shouldn't let herself get too excited. She closed her eyes and slowed her breathing—until she heard someone creaking up the attic steps.

"Katie? Are you still up there?"

"Um, yeah." Katie shut the flaps and turned to block the box with her body, hoping it wouldn't be obvious what she'd been up to.

"Did you find it?" her mom asked.

For a moment, Katie wondered if her mom knew about the box, but then she remembered the reason she'd been sent to the attic in the first place: the Thanksgiving decorations.

"Sorry. I got a little distracted. I was just . . . looking for my snow pants. Since it's finally snowing."

"Oh, sweetheart," said her mom, brushing a tiny flurry of flour from her apron. "I'm not sure you should be playing in the snow today. All that cold can't be good for your heart, and you're so vulnerable to infection."

Now Katie really did look around for the snow gear.

"If I'm building a fort or a snowman or something, I'll be moving around so much I won't even be cold."

Her mom frowned. "Please don't argue with me. If you're too active in all that cold, I imagine it's even worse."

Katie sighed. Her mom was good at so many things—baking and back scratching and singing beautiful songs. But a lot of the time, it seemed like the thing she was best at was imagining the worst.

"Don't worry," said Katie's mom, picking up the Thanksgiving box that must have been in plain sight all along. She steered Katie toward the door. "I've thought of the perfect project for you."

Back in the kitchen, where things were safe and warm but not nearly so exciting, Katie's mom cleared a spot on the end of the table and handed her a stack of paper and a pair of scissors.

"This way we can be in here together. Will you cut the strips for the Thankful Chains?"

Like a good daughter, Katie sat straight down and got to work, cutting sheet after sheet of thick, silvery snowflake paper into strips. Every year, she and her parents made paper chains to count down the days from Thanksgiving to Christmas, and on each little strip, they wrote something they were thankful for. Every night after that, they'd each take a link off their chain and read them aloud. The first year they'd all written each other's names on the very last link—the Christmas Eve link—without even planning it. Now it had become a tradition.

That night, when she and her parents sat around the fire filling out their Thankfuls, Katie started with the easiest ones first. She needed to finish in time to watch for Ana's signal.

I'm thankful for my parents.

Katie sometimes imagined how different her life would be if another family had adopted her, but she never thought about it for long. Even though they hovered a little much, even though her friends always thought they were her grandparents at first because they were so much older, Katie knew she was lucky to have the parents she had.

But when she thought about what must have come before her first memory, Katie began to wonder something else. Not *What if someone else had adopted me?* but *What if I had never been adopted at all?* She wasn't wishing for it, only wondering. Would she still live in Russia? Would they have been able to fix her heart? Would she feel this safe and loved and comfortable?

16

But also:

Would she be allowed to play in the snow? Would her mother send her off on adventures instead of keeping her in the kitchen? Something inside Katie had been stirred up today, and she wasn't entirely sure she wanted it to settle right away. They were only questions, but guilt pricked at her heart all the same.

"Well, this is troubling," said her dad. Katie had always known him with gray hair, but now there were patches of pure white where his glasses hooked around his ears. His paper strips lay blank on his lap, his eyes fixed on the reporter frowning from the TV. "It sounds like the Cold War all over again."

Katie was about to stop her dad and ask what the Cold War was, but he'd trailed off anyway. She followed his gaze across the couch, where she caught her mom doing a very serious head shake and a zip-it-now face. She faked a smile when she realized Katie was watching.

"It wasn't really a war, sweetheart, and it was over long before you were born."

Katie glanced back at the TV, where a map of Russia showed on the screen.

Her mom clicked the mute button and turned to Katie.

"Governments can fight all they like, but there are good people everywhere. You remember that. Now don't trouble yourself with this anymore tonight." She smiled again, but soft this time, and Katie guessed her next words before she even began. "If you know too much, you'll grow old too soon."

Katie didn't want to grow old yet, but she felt ready to grow up, at least a little. Her mom always pulled out that saying at the absolute worst moments. Sometimes Katie even wondered if that was what had happened to her parents—they'd grown old so soon because they knew so much.

Katie's dad taught history at the university, and his new job was the reason they'd had to move. But more important, he was the world's best storyteller and creamy-potato soup maker.

Until Katie had come along, her mom had been a teacher too. She could read stories with all the right voices, and even the hardest math homework didn't seem hard to her. And, of course, she could cook and bake about a thousand amazing things without ever opening a recipe book. Colorful English trifle, peanut-butter pinwheel cookies, homemade doughnuts. Soft rolls that peeled into layers with a sour-sweet kiss of orange glaze on top.

The two of them sat flanking the fireplace, a perfect pair in their matching chairs. And there sat Katie, alone on a couch that could have easily fit all three of them.

Katie tried to ignore the empty spaces beside her as she filled her Thankfuls with all the usuals—house, school, teachers, friends. She squeezed one perfect dot of glue onto each strip and began pressing the links closed, one after another, together and together and together. But as she pressed, her eyes kept darting to the first one she'd written, the last link still waiting to be added to the chain.

There were five seats in this family room, even if only three of them were filled tonight.

Katie's story had a beginning, and even if she didn't remember it, she couldn't just forget it either.

In a brave, brash moment, Katie changed her most important Thankful, making it different by one word and a whole world.

I'm thankful for my birth parents.

Before she could lose her courage, Katie pinched the last strip closed around the end of the chain. She couldn't look at her parents as she laid her Thankfuls on the coffee table.

"Finished already?" asked her dad.

"I have a lot to be thankful for," said Katie.

It was true, but it wasn't quite the truth.

Nobody would read that last link until Christmas Eve, and Katie knew she'd have to force herself not to change it back before then.

"Good girl," said her mom. "Would you hand me the remote? I think I'll do better with a little happy noise in the background. And that means no more news."

Once her mom had found a holiday special, Katie slipped into her coat and shoes and snuck through the back door to wait for Ana's signal. Outside in the frosty night air, she settled herself on the squeaky porch swing. A little grease, she thought, just like the typewriter in the attic. A little love and attention and it would be good as new.

Katie used her toes to gently rock herself back and forth, back and forth, as she watched for the signal. Her two best friends were so different—fearless Ana in Boston, quiet Grace back in Salt Lake—and with the rocking of the swing, she felt the pull of both her worlds.

Ana, Grace. Ana, Grace. First one, then the other, tugging on her heart, each of them a little like a sister. Or at least, how she'd always imagined a sister would be.

The rocking of the swing reminded Katie of her parents too. The mom and dad who had raised and loved her, who had paid for her three expensive surgeries and would find a way to do it again, if they needed to. But every time she swung toward them, there was something deep inside that pulled her back. The barely there memory of wheat-colored hair in a long braid that fell over a soft, safe shoulder. The rattle of paintbrushes against glass rinsing jars, and a smell like Christmas. A voice singing softly in another language, something about a hero and trouble in a strange land. Was it a real memory of Russia? Was that her birth mother's song? Or just something she'd seen in a movie or read in a storybook, once upon a time?

Katie heard her mom's voice inside her. *If you know too much, you'll grow old too soon.*

Were parents even supposed to say things like that? Weren't parents supposed to tell you to learn all you could? Maybe Katie's mom was too old to remember what it felt like to not have all the answers.

Twin lights flickered on in Ana's window, pulling Katie out of her thoughts. Two candles were the signal to meet by the pond, but it seemed too cold and dark for that. Katie watched Ana's empty back porch long enough that she'd begun to wonder if Ana had made a mistake.

Then light spilled from Ana's door and two shapes emerged—Ana and Mikey. They gripped each other's arms and slipped down the slope to the pond.

In the cold. In the dark. But together.

Another pulse of loneliness pulled Katie off the swing and toward her friend. The snow sifted down softly, like the calm first chapter of a big adventure story. The thin layer on the ground barely skimmed the canvas of Katie's sneakers as she started across the backyard and toward the pond, but she knew there would be inches and inches by morning.

As Katie approached, Ana smiled, her eyes bright in the moonlight. "Ever been ice-skating?"

Katie shook her head.

"Ready to try?"

If she stayed near the edge, the worst that could happen was wet socks. Okay, ice-cold wet socks.

But it wasn't even officially winter yet. "Are you sure about this?"

Ana grabbed Mikey's hands and dragged him toward the edge of the pond. "Nope," she said. "That's why this brave soldier's going first."

Mikey may have only been in first grade, but Katie was so small they were almost the same size. Would Ana drag her too?

Katie's toes tingled, and she could feel her nose getting ready to run. She glanced up at the warm golden light of her kitchen window. "I don't know, Ana. We don't even have ice skates."

"Of course not!" Ana said. "We'd chop right through if we were wearing ice skates." She turned to Katie and winked, which was the signal to play along. (With Ana, that was a very important signal to know.)

"Some people," Ana said, "wouldn't even count this as skating, since we don't have skates." She was still trying to coax Mikey to go out ahead of her, which wasn't super courageous but was probably smart, since Mikey was so much smaller. "But I say it counts. Absolutely."

Katie knew Ana always looked out for Mikey, and she usually did her best to play along. Still, this seemed like a terrible idea. "I don't think the ice is thick enough yet."

Mikey darted away from his sister, burrowing under Katie's arm and hiding his face against her coat.

Ana laughed. "Says the girl who just moved here. Boston winters are *cold*, and this one's colder than most already.

Watch." She rolled back her shoulders and stretched a boot onto the ice.

"See?" she said. "Perfectly safe. Come on out." She smiled back at them. "You have to believe!"

But once she put a little weight on her front boot, the ice made a shrieking, cracking sound. Ana tried to pull back, but it was too late. She screamed and grabbed at Katie's sleeve, and the scream made Mikey grab harder onto Katie's coat, and the next thing Katie knew, the three of them were tumbling and shouting and splashing into the dark, icy water.

Ana

Chapter 3

WHEN THE LAST bell set the school free for Thanksgiving break, Ana headed toward the first-grade hall to bundle up her little brother for the cold trudge home. She should've been listening for the hockey buzzer, not the school bell. She should've spent the whole day with her teammates, out on the ice in her favorite hockey tournament of all, the New England Freeze Out.

Ana and Mikey tucked their chins into their coats and

stepped outside. The sun shone so bright in the cold air that colors seemed to fade like an old photograph. Leaving school never even felt like freedom to Ana anymore, and five days away wouldn't be much of a vacation without any hockey to look forward to. This break was going to stink worse than cafeteria trash. It was going to bite worse than great whites. The fourth week of November was supposed to be spent skipping school to play in Springfield, shoveling down turkey and pie, then skating it off at the rink with her dad.

Last year, when Ana had been the only ten-year-old to make the twelve-and-under elite hockey team, her dad had actually come to the tournament, and everyone had freaked out to see a real live NHL player there. Then Ana and her dad had spent the whole day after Thanksgiving at the Bruins' practice arena, working on her slap shot and her puck handling while Mikey watched movies and ate popcorn in the stands. Ana had even gotten extra-good Hanukkah presents, because her mom had been kid-free for Black Friday shopping.

This year, there probably wouldn't be any presents, and there definitely wouldn't be any hockey.

Partly because Ana hadn't even tried out for the league.
Mostly because her dad was gone.

"Come on, Mikey," Ana said, slowing her pace to match her little brother's. First he'd raced ahead without waiting for Katie, and now that Katie had turned down her own street, he was barely moving. Sometimes Ana felt like she spent half her life telling her little brother to hurry up.

Mikey dropped to his knees in the snow.

Ana sighed. "What's the problem now?"

"I lost it," he said. His chin trembled as he held up his hand to show her one lonely marble. "I lost the other one."

Whenever he could, Mikey held the two smooth swirls of orange glass, one in each hand, and tapped them against each other. For months, he'd been obsessed with pairing things up. Shampoo and conditioner, salt and pepper, peanut butter and honey, always lined up and touching like they were getting their picture taken. She'd leave her room for two seconds and come back to find her shoes that way, instead of in a heap like she'd left them.

But his favorite pair was the orange marbles. And now one was missing.

Ana scanned the sidewalk and the ditch. "Geez, is that all? I'm surprised you can hold on to anything with those fat mittens." It only took about five seconds for her to find the marble in the gutter and drop it back into Mikey's hand. "Put them in your pocket, okay?"

Before he put them away, Mikey tapped the marbles against each other with a soft *chik-chik*. "The Flyers need my good luck. They're playing Pittsburgh tonight."

"Holy smokes," Ana said. "How many times do I have to tell you? I do not give one single rip about the Philadelphia Flyers."

Except she did. Of course she did. Ana had been following the Flyers all season, because that was her dad's team now. She slid Mikey's backpack off his shoulders and looped it around her front like a chest guard. Even though she hadn't played in months, Ana's brain still found its way back to hockey.

Ana nudged Mikey forward, trying to think of anything that might get him to move a little faster. "We've got to check on Mom. Hey, maybe it's a good day. Maybe she made cookies!"

Ana's mom hadn't actually made much of anything

for months. The whole reason Ana had told her mom she didn't want to try out for hockey this season was so she could watch Mikey while her mom went to work, but now her mom didn't even leave the house. She just wore her workout clothes all day without ever actually going to the gym.

But there were memories inside Ana that came to the surface sometimes, like making sugar cookie turkeys last year with candy-corn tail feathers. There were still moments when her mind wouldn't believe that everything had changed.

Ana fished out her key and creaked the door open. Her "hello" echoed hollow through the house, unanswered.

Not a good day, then.

She led Mikey through the maze of mess to the kitchen. The house was never clean anymore unless Ana was the one to clean it, and that didn't happen very often.

Mikey unzipped his backpack and started unloading everything onto the counter. Crumpled worksheets, fruit snack wrappers, an unidentified art project with colorful feathers.

"Stop," Ana said. "You're making it worse."

Mikey ignored her and kept digging.

"There it is!" His face lit up as he pulled a paper chain from the bag.

"What is that? Mikey, did you make a Christmas countdown?"

Mikey rolled his eyes. "We're Jewish, Ana."

As if she'd forgotten. As if she hadn't reminded the teacher when she was in first grade and her own class was supposed to make red-and-green Christmas countdowns. Instead, Ana had been given a "special assignment" that was just the first Hanukkah coloring page her teacher could find on the internet.

"It's a winter-break countdown," Mikey explained. "My teacher made one too. He's super excited for winter break. Every day I get to take off one circle, and when it's gone, hallelujah! The orange circle is Thanksgiving and the blue ones are Hanukkah. He showed us lots of ways to make them with the different colors." He scanned the kitchen. "Where's Mom? I want to show her!"

Ana sighed. "I don't think she's . . ."

"Hey!" Mikey scooted a dirty plate aside and climbed onto the counter. "There's a note!"

A note. *Just like that day last summer.* Ana tried to swipe it, but Mikey held it close. "I can read it."

It was a lie—Mikey was only in first grade and not the greatest reader. But Ana let him give it a shot.

"Dear Awesome Kids," he started, and Ana knew he was faking it. She'd seen Mikey spell awesome: *O-S-U-M*.

Mikey squinted at the words. "Eat anything you want as long as Mikey gets the biggest piece. And he can play with Ana's hockey gear and wear her dinosaur slippers. Love, Mom. The End."

"Don't lie, Mikey," Ana said.

Don't be like him.

But she didn't say that part. She just snagged the note from Mikey's fingers and scanned it, surprised by how much he had gotten right.

Hi, my awesome kids,

Ran to the airport to pick up a surprise. ~~Clean up after yourselves.~~ Clean up as much as you can. I should get home right after you do.

Love, Mom

Ana touched the last two words and felt a gentle brush of hope. If her mom had left the house, it might be a good day after all. She reread the first sentence, wondering why she'd felt a hint of something even better there.

Then she got it: *a surprise from the airport.* People didn't go to the airport to pick up packages. They went to the airport to pick up people.

Maybe Dad was coming back.

The last time Ana had seen her dad was three months ago at that same airport, when he'd stayed behind for training camp while the rest of the family went off for two weeks at the lake. He'd hugged Ana extra tight at the curb that day and given her one of the game pucks from his collection.

As she'd held the puck and turned it over on the plane, running her fingers across the cool, black rubber, she'd thought, *He gave me this because he loves me. He gave me this because I'm his favorite.* She hadn't even for one second thought, *He gave me this because he's leaving.*

When they'd returned from the lake, just a few days before school started, they'd waited for him at the curb for over an hour. "I sent him an email," her mom had said, like that was a normal way for families to meet up after weeks apart. She'd called again and again, but he hadn't answered, and finally they'd given up and gotten a ride-share driver to take them home.

When they'd walked through the door that day, the house had felt empty and quiet and way too clean. Like something had been erased. The only thing on the counter at all had been his note, which Ana's mom had still never let her read.

Not that it mattered; Ana knew the important parts. Her dad had signed with Philadelphia, and he didn't want them to follow. After Mikey had found out, he'd cried every time Ana or her mom left the room, afraid they'd leave for real like his dad had. Ana and her mom had slept on either side of Mikey that first night, all three of them piled into her mom's bed, crying together. Ana was the only one who hadn't cried almost every day since. The next morning, she'd woken first and hidden the puck under her mattress, too mad and hurt to hold it or even look at it, but needing to be near it all the same.

Now, Ana read her mom's note again. *Clean up as much as you can.* Maybe they were supposed to clean up so it would look exactly like it had when he'd left, so he'd feel like he hadn't been gone so long. Like he hadn't missed out on Mikey's soccer season and Ana quitting hockey and everything else that had happened since August.

But maybe things were coming back together, and that was the reason her mom had left an almost-normal note. Maybe they'd all be moving to Philadelphia. Maybe it wasn't too late for her dad to keep some of his promises.

"Mikey!" she shouted. "Help me clean up! Or at least don't make any new messes. They'll be here any minute."

Wrappers crinkled in the pantry.

"Mikey, please!" When Ana opened the pantry door, Mikey had climbed the shelves like a ladder and was clutching a bright orange bag.

"Check it out! Cheetos!" It had been so long since they'd had good snacks that Ana was tempted.

"And orange is good luck for the Flyers. Catch, Ana!"

Mikey tossed the bag down, and Ana caught it.

"Catch again!"

Before Ana could even drop the bag, Mikey jumped from his perch. He knocked her backward, landing on top of her as the bag exploded with a bang between them.

Mikey laughed like a maniac as he scooped a handful of orange puffs off the floor and shoved them into his mouth. "We're a Cheetos sandwich!" he said, sitting on Ana's belly and showering her with curls.

Ana rolled him off her and started finger-sweeping Cheetos into a pile. "These are Dad's, you nerd, and he's coming home right now! You're going to be in so much trouble!"

Mikey tugged at her arm. "Dad's coming home? Did the Bruins get him back?"

Ana hadn't meant to say it out loud until she was totally sure. She brushed Mikey's hands away and shook her head. "I don't know. It might only be for Thanksgiving. Just help me!" She dropped a handful of Cheetos back into the bag.

After that, Ana took her job seriously for as long as she could. But the hope had found its way inside her and turned into something like happiness. Before long, even the mess seemed funny, and the whole thing turned into a game. She and Mikey were both stuffing their cheeks with Cheetos and laughing so hard they didn't hear the car in the driveway or the key in the lock. The first thing they heard was their mom's voice.

"Ana! Mikey!" she called. "We're home!"

Right then, Mikey grabbed the bag and dumped all

the Cheetos they'd gathered back out and over his face.

An icy draft crawled across Ana's skin as a tall figure appeared in the doorway.

It wasn't Dad.

It was Babushka.

Ana

Chapter 4

ANA'S MOUTH DROPPED open. Her last two handfuls of Cheetos fell to the floor, but her eyes were stuck on the figure in front of her. It was like spotting a long, wiry ear hair or watching a croc attack on TV—totally horrifying, but she couldn't look away.

There she was: Babushka. The hope that had been growing inside Ana shriveled like Babushka's gray, wrinkly flesh.

Mikey scrambled behind Ana, sniffling and whimpering against the back of her shirt.

Most kids weren't afraid of their own grandmas, but most grandmas weren't as witch-like as Babushka. She was tall and thin, but she must have been taller once, because she always curved forward a little, like she was trying to get a better look at you.

Ana had expected a terrible Thanksgiving break, but Babushka brought her own creepy brand of awful. Her hair was white and pulled into a loose bun on top of her head, but there were always strands sticking straight out. It gave Ana the feeling that lightning might strike at any second.

"Babushka is here for Thanksgiving break," said Ana's mom. "Isn't that wonderful?" The way she said it, Ana knew she wasn't quite sure of the answer herself.

"Where's Dad?" Mikey was full-out crying now.

Not again.

"Mikhail," Babushka said, even though nobody who knew him at all called him anything but Mikey. "You sound like osyol. Come hug your babushka. We are supposed to enjoy hugging, no?"

Babushka held out her skinny arms, but Mikey stared

at her like she was speaking another language instead of just talking with a Russian accent.

Ana stepped forward to get her hug over with, but Babushka waved her away. "You are too old for hugs." She frowned. "You fix your hair with eyes closed?"

Ana touched her hair, and even with just her fingertips, she could tell what a mess it was. It wasn't like she cared, mostly. But she had to admit that when she saw Katie's perfect braids every morning, a part of her wanted to have somebody take care of her like that once in a while.

Babushka nudged her luggage forward with the toe of her boot. "Show your old babushka how you love her by bringing her suitcase upstairs. But first, clean up this mess." She waved a gnarled hand at the Cheetos like she was casting a spell, and Ana almost expected them to turn into a swarm of cockroaches or something.

Ana's mom opened the broom closet and stared inside. She stared a lot lately, especially on bad days, like it took every ounce of energy and every inch of concentration just to do regular things like sweep the floor. But before she could gather enough of either one, Babushka tugged her aside.

"The children will clean the mess. Take me to my

room, doch. I need to lie down after such a journey. The pilot was terrible. His landing rattled my teeth loose. And the stingy woman with the snacks! One tiny bag of tiny pretzels!"

Ana winced as Babushka's boot made an unmistakable Cheetos crunch. Babushka hobbled over to a bar stool and leaned against it as she wiped orange dust from her boot. "My son cannot live in a mess like this."

"Your son doesn't live here anymore." Ana's mom spoke with so much hurt in her voice it sounded like he'd left them all over again.

Babushka waved a hand. "Yes, he plays for Firebirds now. We will fix this. We will fix all of this."

"Flyers," Mikey insisted. Of all that was wrong in this moment, he cared about the name of the hockey team? Babushka eyed him, but Mikey didn't back down.

"Flyers," he repeated. "Not Firebirds."

Babushka leaned toward them.

"Your father told you of firebird, yes? I told him this story a hundred times when he was a little boy. Did he tell you also of Baba Yaga? Of Vasilisa?"

Ana didn't know who those guys were and she didn't care, but Babushka just went for it.

"I will tell you the story as my babushka told it to me, and her babushka before her. Long ago in Russia there lived a kind, brave girl named Vasilisa. Her mother loved her very much. But love was not enough to heal the mother's terrible cough or cool her terrible fever, and she died a tragic, painful death."

"Wait!" Mikey looked at his own mom with big, sad eyes. "She *died*?"

Ana's mom hated stories where the moms were dead or pure evil. She should have been standing up to Babushka, but she looked like she'd already given up. Like today had already been more than she could handle.

"It wasn't her fault," she said. She closed her eyes. "Let me help you upstairs, Babushka."

Babushka thought about that for a second. "Yes, I am still tired," she said. "But do not worry, Mikhail. I will finish the story later. You will like it. Real fairy tales do not all have perfect endings. Only American fairy tales." Her mouth curved into a smile as she turned to Ana. "Soon Vasilisa will meet the witch."

Then Babushka followed her daughter-in-law upstairs, leaving Ana with not just the Cheetos mess, but the upset-Mikey mess too.

Fantastic.

"What happened after that?" Mikey asked. "Ana, what's the end of the story?"

"The mom comes back to life," Ana said, wishing things could really be that way. "They live happily ever after. Now start helping."

What a disaster. Ana couldn't let herself act like a kid, even for a few minutes, or everything fell apart.

It wasn't only Cheetos cluttering the floor, though. There were crumbs and scraps and dried-up bits of mac and cheese. *This is not my mess to clean up*, Ana kept thinking.

With every swipe of the broom, Ana pulled a little harder and got a little madder. Ever since her mom had gotten sad, Ana had been trying so hard to help. Trying not to miss the game and the friends she'd given up.

All that trying and everything kept getting worse. How could her mom have brought Babushka here? Ana didn't believe for one second that Babushka could bring her dad back. He'd always avoided the old lady just as much as the rest of them.

Ana dumped the pile into the trash. Most of the mess was gone, but it wouldn't ever be clean for long. She felt

Mikey staring as she shoved the broom and dustpan back into the closet.

"What?" she asked, shutting the door with as much slam as she thought she'd get away with. "What do you need now?"

He sniffled and wiped his nose along the cuff of his sleeve. "Is Mom going to die? Is that why Babushka told that story? Is that why she's here?"

A small twist of fear tightened inside Ana, but she wouldn't give it any attention, so it couldn't come true. Ana knelt to look Mikey straight in the face. "She's going to be fine. Stories like that aren't real."

Mikey climbed onto the table and sat cross-legged, staring at her. "So stories aren't real?"

"Not that kind."

He slumped down and propped his chin in his hands. "That's the kind with magic, though. And happy endings."

"I guess."

"So magic and happy endings aren't real?"

Right then, Ana had a hard time believing they were. But first grade was way too young to give up.

"Hey," she said. "I didn't mean that. They're real. Good things still happen." She ran a stream of water across a paper towel and wiped Mikey's face as her mind stretched toward anything that might give her brother a little hope.

Then she had it. Before she could talk herself out of it, Ana grabbed Mikey's hand and dragged him past Babushka's suitcase and upstairs toward the one thing she owned that he didn't know about.

Ana sat Mikey down on her bed. "Close your eyes," she said.

Mikey squeezed his eyes shut so tight his mouth molded into a fake smile. "Like this?"

"Just like that." Ana slid her hand under the mattress and found the lump she'd hidden in the bottom corner. "When I say 'three,' open them up."

Mikey's eyes popped open. "You said three!" He glanced at the scuffed-up hockey puck in Ana's hands and leaned over to try to see behind her back. "Where's the surprise? Can I eat it?"

Ana sighed and held the puck in front of Mikey, cupping it gently, like a bird's nest. "Remember when Dad scored that overtime goal against the Red Wings last season? When we all went to Detroit together?"

Mikey pushed the puck away. "*Preseason*, Ana. Those games don't even count. And it has a Red Wings logo. He never even put it in a case like the others." Mikey scooted back against the wall and started clicking his marbles together. "When we left for the lake, he asked me if I wanted it, but I said no."

Ana weighed the puck in her hands. It was heavier and dirtier and much more ordinary than she'd remembered. *He only offered it to me because Mikey didn't want it.*

When her dad had scored that goal, it had sure felt like it counted, but now she realized Mikey was right. They used a dozen pucks in an average game, and the Bruins played eighty-two games a year. That meant almost a thousand pucks, and this one was preseason. How had she ever thought an ugly piece of rubber was something special?

The puck was totally ordinary, just like Ana was without hockey. Her dad was gone, and he hadn't even cared enough to give her anything that mattered. Her mom was disappearing too, but not in ways Ana could fully understand. Babushka was here to ruin Thanksgiving. Mikey's crying might get worse.

No. Ana had to shake this off. She couldn't be ordinary. It couldn't get worse. She ran her thumbs across the puck's dents and scratches. Even if there weren't happy endings or real magic in the world, Mikey couldn't know it yet. If she could pretty much be Mikey's parent, she could be his fairy godmother too.

Or something like that.

"Hey," she said. "I have a secret. Dad didn't know it, but he left us with the best puck of all."

Mikey held the marbles still. He gave the puck a closer look.

Ana lowered her voice. "Remember how you asked about magic and happy endings?"

Before Mikey could ask any questions, Ana spoke her lie. Except it wouldn't really be a lie if she could somehow make it come true.

"This puck is magic."

Something flickered inside Ana, and she almost believed her own words for a second.

Mikey sat straight up and grabbed the puck from Ana's hands. "If you're trying to trick me, I'll tell Mom."

Ana didn't even know if that was true, since neither of them told their mom much of anything anymore. She missed the days when her mom had been the one to make things magical and her dad had been the one to make things fun. If she had a wish, she'd wish to have that back.

She closed Mikey's hands around the puck and wrapped hers around his.

"Mom doesn't know, and you can't tell her. Dad doesn't know either. But some pucks are. The ones with an M-shaped scratch, just like this one." Ana nudged Mikey's fingers aside and showed him four deep gashes that made a perfect *M*.

Or a perfect *W*, like, *What the heck are you doing, Ana?*

"*M* for magic," Mikey whispered. He touched the puck like it might be a treasure, so Ana kept going.

"When you have a problem and you don't know what to do, just hold it between your hands, like this. You whisper what you need help with, and it'll fix the problem for you. The only catch is, I have to be with you, since it belongs to me." If this didn't work, Mikey would figure out pretty quick that there wasn't any magic, and things would be worse than ever.

Mikey still stared at the chunk of dark, dirty rubber, like he was trying to decide whether he believed.

"Come on," Ana said. "Try it out. Tell it what's wrong."

Mikey closed his eyes and curled his fingers around the puck. "I don't know how to stop crying all the time. If I never cried again, maybe Jarek would leave me alone." He rested his forehead on the logo, and his voice dropped to a feathery whisper. "I just want to have happy days again."

Ana rested her chin on top of Mikey's head. She could make this happen. Not that she believed in wishes—not really. But she believed in work, and she sure as heck believed in herself.

"You will have happy days again, buddy. Watch." She took the puck from him and held it close to her mouth. "Now I give it a kiss and whisper the magic spell. But you can't listen!"

Mikey plugged his ears as Ana gave the puck a quick peck. She pretended to whisper, but really, she was blowing all the warm air from deep inside her onto the puck.

"There," she said, holding it out to Mikey again. He unplugged his ears, and she nodded down at the puck. "Feel that spot, right on top? How it's a little warmer and a little wet?" Mikey touched the puck, and his eyes grew wide.

"That's the magic waking up," Ana said. "That means it's going to work. But your problem was a big one, so it might take a while."

Mikey thought about this. Then his face brightened, and he grabbed the puck back from Ana.

"Hey, I know another one that could be faster! I wish Dad could take me skating. Tonight."

"Geez, Mikey," said Ana, taking the puck from him. "It's not a magic lamp."

Mikey's face scrunched up again, so Ana grabbed him into a tight, safe hug.

"Okay, okay. You're right. That's exactly the right size of a problem to fix. But I just remembered you can't make wishes about other people—that's one of the rules. Sorry." Ana pulled back and looked him right in the eye. "Even if Dad won't be there, though, we're going skating tonight."

After an uncomfortable dinner of onion stew (Babushka's favorite) and being told how much colder winters were in Russia (cold enough to freeze onion stew), it was finally time for skating.

Ana went up to her room to send Katie their super-secret signal. "One if by land," she recited as she shuffled through the junk under her bed, "two if by sea."

Katie had come up with the idea weeks ago when the whole fifth grade had gone on a field trip to the Freedom Trail. They'd lined up two by two and followed the rows of red brick down narrow roads to the Old North Church.

"We should do that," she'd whispered as the tour guide told the story of Paul Revere. "Candles in the window for signals."

They'd worked it all out on the bus ride back to school. One candle meant *See if you can come over!* (Which was always traveling by land.) And two candles meant *Meet me by the pond.*

Ana definitely didn't want Katie showing up at her door tonight, and the pond was where they needed to be anyway. Two candles, then. A pair. Mikey would approve.

Ana twisted the plastic flames to turn on the electric candles. As she positioned them on the windowsill, she heard Babushka complaining about all the little things that were wrong with the guest room.

Perfect. That would keep the grown-ups busy for a while.

Still, Ana's heart raced as she and Mikey tucked their gloves and scarves under the edges of their coats and tip-toed to the back door.

When they were safe outside, Mikey stopped and looked up at Ana. "Are you sure it'll work?"

"Do you trust the puck?" Ana asked as Katie's shadowy

shape stepped toward them. "If you don't trust, it can't work."

"I trust the puck," Mikey said, slipping his small hand in hers. "And I trust you."

But once they'd all gathered at the pond, Ana suddenly wished she had a reason to wait. As her best friend and little brother stood, huddled together and looking at her so hopefully, she asked another question deep inside. *Do you trust yourself, Ana Petrova?*

The answer had to be yes. It had to be, or none of this would work.

So when Mikey didn't dare step onto the ice, Ana put her own boot out first. "See?" she said. "Perfectly safe. Come on out. You have to believe!" She held her breath and shifted her weight.

The ice creaked and cracked. Ana made a desperate grab at Katie's sleeve. Then a shock of cold screamed through her, and they were all in the pond.

Katie

Chapter 5

KATIE CRASHED INTO the icy pond with Mikey on top of her. The cold stole her breath and seemed to stop her heart for a long moment. Her mind froze too, then woke with a sudden shock.

Keep your chest out of the water.

Keep your heart warm.

The thoughts tumbled through Katie's head as the

water rushed in at her waist and soaked through her shoes. She hoisted Mikey off her lap and toward the shore, but the struggle sank her deeper as shards of ice sliced at her wrists. At the edge of her vision, at the edge of the pond, a woman appeared with wild, white hair and a dark, old-fashioned coat. Was Katie imagining things? Could the cold be making her crazy?

Another scream cut through the air from Katie's back porch, and time snapped back to normal. Katie scrambled to her feet, her frozen clothes sucked against her skin. She tried to stop her chattering teeth as her mom stumbled the hundred feet down the slope.

Mikey, she remembered. But he was already safe on shore, kneeling to reach out to her. Before Katie could get to him, the old woman gathered Mikey under her coat and hurried him away, muttering words Katie could almost hear, almost understand, as she waded out of the icy water. Ana stomped out of the pond, splashing and fake-cursing, and raced after Mikey.

The ends of Katie's hair and the canvas of her shoes had frozen stiff by the time her mom had rushed her back up to the house, murmuring a prayer under her breath.

"I'll be speaking with Ana about this too," she said, grabbing a towel from the bathroom cupboard. "I can't believe she'd lure you down to the pond like that." She sat Katie in front of the fire and draped the towel over her shoulders, then began tugging at her sneakers.

Katie closed her eyes and let the warmth of the fire spread over her for a few seconds before she answered. "I can take my own shoes off, Mom. And she didn't lure me. I went down to say hi."

Her mom planted her hands on her hips. "You went down there in antarctic weather, in the dark, without wearing your boots or telling your mother? Just to say hi to a friend you'd spent all day with?" She brushed Katie's hands aside and yanked at her wet socks, but they only stretched like taffy.

Katie took over the sock situation, hoping to keep this from turning into a fight. But when she looked up, her mom's eyes filled with tears as she reached to warm Katie's frozen toes. "What if you'd had a cardiac event? You're not built for shocks like that, honey. Your heart's not strong enough."

"I'm sorry, Mom," Katie said. "I won't do it again."

Her mom lifted Katie's chin with her fingertips. "You promise me? No more sneaking around? No more trips to the pond?"

"I promise." Katie realized this never would have turned into a fight, because she never dared stand up to her mom anyway.

After hot cider and a hotter bath, Katie's mom sent her straight to bed. But Katie's dad snuck in after she'd burrowed safe and dry under the covers.

"You know," he said with a smile, "a wise woman once said, 'If you know too much, you'll grow old too soon.'" He pulled up a chair next to the bed and eased down into it.

"Yeah, I guess."

"But you know what I always say? If you don't know enough, you end up with ice water in your britches."

Katie laughed. "You *always* say that?"

Her dad smoothed the hair from her face. "I'll talk to her."

"About what?"

"The kids. The pond. The things you think you're ready to know."

Katie squeezed her dad's hand. *The things I think*

I'm ready to know. She imagined the box in the attic and thought of each of the beautiful things she'd held only a few hours ago.

"But for tonight," her dad said, "we have a tradition to keep."

Every year, on the night of the first snowfall, Katie's dad brought out his old brown journal and read her the story he'd scrawled on its small, lined pages. Katie settled deeper under the covers and closed her eyes as her dad's voice, somehow both scratchy and smooth, told the tale.

"*The Snow Child,*" he began, and they shared a smile.

"Once there was a couple who could not have children of their own. Year after year, they hoped for a baby, and the husband ached as he watched his wife suffer. He yearned to hear her laugh again, and to hear the sound echoed by the sweet laughter of a son or daughter.

"One winter morning, the man stood at the kitchen window and thought this very thing. Although his gaze seemed to rest on the forest outside, he barely noticed the snow bending the branches and blanketing the ground. Then a single flake, weaving its way through the air before him, caught his attention. Suddenly, the snow was all he could see. Suddenly, he knew exactly what to do.

"The old man bundled into his woolen mittens and work-roughened boots. He rushed outside and gathered the snow in great armfuls, then packed it carefully into a tight mound. He shaped and brushed and pushed until his fingers were stiff with cold and use. But even then, he removed his mittens and began carving the details with his fingers."

Katie watched her own father's fingers turn the pages. *These were the hands that helped me learn to write my name,* she thought. *The hands that held mine the first time I danced.*

Then her father's voice pulled her back into the story.

"The snow hid the sound of the old woman's slow, careful footsteps as she came to where her husband worked.

"'Oh,' she whispered. 'There you are.'

"But she wasn't looking at the old man. She was looking at the child he had formed.

"The girl stood before them in a flowing dress—white, of course—with hair made from strands of silk grass, sparkling with frost."

Katie thought of the frozen ends of her own hair earlier tonight as her father turned the page.

"The old woman's eyes filled with tears as her one great wish almost seemed possible again. She reached out and cradled the curve of the girl's cheek in her wrinkled hand. 'If only you were real.' With a tight grip on her husband's arm to keep her old bones steady, the woman leaned forward and kissed the snow child's other cheek.

"They were all connected then, and the warmth of the old woman's hand and lips seeped between the packed flakes and spread through the snow child. Deep inside the child, a single snowflake shifted, and it was enough.

"The child's heart began to beat.

"*Tuc-tuc, tuc-tuc.*"

Katie's dad reached over and patted the quilt in a gentle rhythm, and Katie's own pulse quickened.

"With each beat, a little warmth and color spread from her chest.

"*Tuc-tuc, tuc-tuc.*

"The kind old couple held each other and watched and waited and prayed. It couldn't be happening. And yet . . .

"*Tuc-tuc, tuc-tuc.*

"The color spread to the girl's fingers and feet, to her chin and cheeks. Her eyes blinked once, and again. She looked from the old man to the old woman and drew a deep breath, and with that first breath, she spoke.

"'Oh,' she whispered. 'There you are.'

"The little family rushed together and collapsed, laughing and crying all at once, right there in the snow. The old couple marveled at their daughter, and she marveled at all the world around her. And just like that, they were a family."

When the story ended, Katie found her mom standing in the doorway with a smile on her face that told Katie all was forgiven, if not forgotten. She came and sat on the foot of Katie's bed, and it felt right to have them all together in her small room while the snow landed, flake upon flake, blanketing the world outside.

"I love that story," she said. "Did your dad tell you it's an old, old story, but he made it new for you?"

Katie nodded.

"And has he ever told you about the first time he told it to you?"

This time, Katie shook her head. The story felt so familiar that she hadn't ever thought about the first time, even though there must have been one.

"We were all together in a room smaller than this." A happy shiver snuck through Katie as her mom continued. "But we were in an orphanage, halfway around the world. As soon as we saw you, we knew."

Knew what? Katie wondered. But the story was already moving on.

"You were fast asleep," her mom said. "And we were so tired too, after flying through the night to get to you. But I took you in my arms and rocked you, in and out of a patch of light from the one little window in the room."

Katie's mom held out her hand, and her dad passed the little journal to her. "Your dad knelt right in front of us and turned to these very same pages. 'You hold her so she gets to know you,' he said, 'and I'll tell her a story, so she gets to know me.' His glasses kept sliding down his nose, and every time, he'd peek down at you before he slid them back up."

Katie's parents smiled at each other, and Katie could hear the catch in her mom's voice when she spoke again.

"Right when he finished, the sun broke through the clouds for a moment, and you squinted in the light. You turned your little face up to me and said, 'Mama?'"

Katie had never heard that part of the story. Thanks to her dad, she knew exactly the right way to end it.

"And just like that," she said, "we were a family."

☆

Later that night, Katie heard thin patches of her parents' conversation through her bedroom wall.

"I think she's ready to know more than we're telling her. She's growing up, you know."

Her dad was keeping his promise.

"Oh, I know." Her mom's voice found its way through the wall much more clearly than her dad's. "But you're still reading her the same story you did the day we met her. You don't even dare tell her how a fairy tale ends!"

That's not the end? Katie felt a little sick. What happened to the snow child that her parents wouldn't want her to know about? And what else had they been keeping from her? She thought of the news story—how they'd muted it and talked around it without actually explaining anything. How their final answer had been to just change the channel.

After that, Katie's parents went into the bathroom, and she couldn't hear the conversation at all over the splashing of water in the sink and the buzz of electric toothbrushes. But the sounds of their routine eased her worry a little, and her eyelids had grown heavy by the time they ambled back into their bedroom.

Her dad's voice drifted through the wall once more, low and unsure. "Maybe you're right. Maybe it's too much." He paused, and Katie heard his footsteps pacing on the other side of the wall. "Shouldn't I at least tell her the rest of the story?"

Then her mom's voice came, final but not unkind. "Not yet. When it's time."

When will it be time? Katie wondered. But she had grown too tired to follow that one last question as it floated across her mind to the soft rhythm of her heart.

Katie

Chapter 6

THE NEXT MORNING, Katie woke to the sound of voices. Her mom again . . . and someone else.

Ana. In Katie's kitchen before she was even awake.

Katie wiggled her feet into her slippers and padded downstairs toward the voices, but also toward whatever her mom was baking that smelled so good. Hopefully there was something she could at least taste test before Thanksgiving.

Katie snuck up and wrapped an arm around her mom's waist. But instead of pulling her close, her mom stiffened. "Oh! You're awake. Did you see how much snow we got last night?"

Out of the corner of her eye, Katie caught her mom hiding a small piece of paper in her apron pocket. She'd seen Ana use the old "Look over there!" trick on Mikey plenty of times, but she'd never realized her mom used it on her.

"Hey!" Ana said. "I've got something for you." She held out a pair of scratchy-looking red socks. "Knitted them myself to say sorry. They're nice and warm." Katie was ready for Ana's play-along wink that time. Ana had never knitted a stitch in her life.

Katie's mom frowned at the socks like she almost approved. "They're very nice. But no socks are warm when they're wet, young lady. You and Katie stay off that pond."

Sometimes Katie wondered if her mom had saved up all her mothering all those years, and now it came out in every direction.

But Ana didn't seem to mind. "Yes, Mrs. Burton. Will do."

"Is your brother okay?"

"Yes, ma'am. He's all dried out and warmed up, back to his usual pesky self."

"Glad to hear it." She held up her flour-coated hands. "Could you girls grab the cloves from the cupboard? And the nutmeg? I'm a mess."

Katie opened the spice cupboard and scanned the shelves. She found the nutmeg pretty quickly in the neat rows of plastic canisters and passed it to Ana. Eventually she found the cloves too, buried in a little glass bottle with a handwritten label.

"Got it!" she called. She turned around to find Ana with her nose hovering over the nutmeg.

"Mmm. Don't you love it?"

Katie inhaled and agreed—the nutmeg did smell nice. It reminded her of making pumpkin-chocolate cookies back in the Salt Lake kitchen. She was still savoring it when Ana popped the cork out of the little clove bottle. "Let's try that one."

But before Ana had even finished speaking, the smell of the cloves had found its way inside Katie, all by itself for the first time in forever. She closed her eyes and inhaled again, and a picture formed of being carried inside a small, warm house after being pulled on a sled. And she knew—*this* was the smell of her birth mother, whom she hadn't remembered this clearly in so, so long.

She almost didn't trust herself. How could she know so surely and so suddenly? But she did. It was almost like that time last spring when they'd woken up to snow in May. There was certainly no arguing about it or pretending it wasn't there when it lay before you so clearly.

Her mom wiped off her hands and held them open before the girls. "If you're finished sticking your noses in my spices, ladies, cut yourselves a piece of gingerbread and scoot."

Katie let her mom take the little bottle of cloves from her hands, but she soaked in the look of it, in case she wanted to find it later. She cut two squares of gingerbread and set them on two small plates. As she finished smoothing the whipped cream on top, Ana started pulling her away.

"Come on," she said. She nodded at Katie's mom like they shared a secret. "Your mom has important baking to do. Let's eat in your room."

Ana nodded at the Thankful Chains on her way up the stairs. "Hey, Mikey made one of those at school. What are you guys counting down to?"

Katie nearly tripped on the bottom step. She'd forgotten about the dangerous thing she'd written, for a few hours anyway.

"Until my family might fall apart."

Ana stopped. "What?"

Katie hadn't meant to say it out loud. "Never mind." She trudged up the steps. "It's just counting down until Christmas. That's all." She remembered what she'd been wanting to ask Ana.

"Who was that old lady at the pond last night?"

Ana turned at the top of the steps. "You mean your mom?"

"My mom's not that old," Katie said, even though that wasn't totally true. "The one with you and Mikey."

"Hmm, didn't notice her," Ana said as she led the way to Katie's room. But there was something shifty about the way she said it. She sat at Katie's desk and turned to her plate. "Mmm, gingerbread. You really do live in a fairy tale over here, huh?"

Something like that, Katie thought. But she let Ana get away with changing the subject.

The girls ate their gingerbread together, then spent the rest of the day doing things that were guaranteed not to get them into trouble. Ana showed Katie how to make paper snowflakes the right way, with six sides instead of eight. Katie showed Ana how to fold paper stars, wanting to feel as close and comfortable with Ana as she had with Grace. She thought of the words Grace wrote on the bottom of every letter.

Remember this truth: you are not alone.

Katie had friends in Boston now, and of course she had her parents too, but she did feel so alone here sometimes. There had to be a way to feel connected again. Maybe if she just talked about Grace with Ana.

"One time," she said, "my friend Grace and I told our secrets and wrote them inside the paper stars."

Ana thought for a second. "Okay," she said. "You go first."

Katie shrank back into her chair. "I didn't mean we had to do it. And I don't have any secrets. Not really."

Ana gave her a look. "Everybody has secrets. Okay,

fine. I'll go first." She closed her eyes and took a deep breath, like she was about to swim wall to wall underwater. "I used to be a hockey player like my dad. Now that the season's started, it kills me to think about everybody else on the ice while I'm just sitting around here doing nothing after school."

Like me. Katie tried not to seem wounded, but it stung to know that's how Ana thought of their afternoons together. She swallowed and tried to focus on her friend. Even though she'd never been able to play sports, Katie knew plenty about leaving behind something you loved.

"Couldn't you start playing again?"

Ana flopped back on Katie's bed and stared at the ceiling. "It's too late for this season, and my mom couldn't handle it anyway. She's a mess. It feels like my dad was the only reason she cared about anything."

Was that what happened to my birth parents? Katie wondered. *Did she stop caring about me when he stopped caring about her? How many different ways do families fall apart?*

Ana sighed. "I mean, I know my mom loved us. *Loves* us. If I could just figure out how to pull her back from wherever she's gone, we'd be okay. Then maybe he'd come back too. We're not the kind of kids you give up on."

Katie lost her breath for a second. Ana didn't know about her adoption. She didn't mean anything by it. Did she?

Ana propped up on one elbow to face Katie. "So there you go: my biggest secret is my messed-up family. Not much of a secret, huh?" She sat up. "Okay, your turn. Tell me all your darkest secrets. You owe me at least two for that."

Katie didn't want to tell Ana about her heart because it made her weak.

She didn't want to tell Ana about her adoption because it made her whole family seem wrong today, even when it had seemed perfectly right last night.

But she'd have to say something. With every second that ticked by, she knew Ana would be expecting something bigger, but the real secrets seemed to burrow deeper inside her.

"I sucked my thumb," she finally said.

"So?" Ana asked. "I did too. Same with Mikey."

"I sucked my thumb until I was in first grade." In reality, it was more like third grade, and every once in a while, she'd still wake up with her thumb in her mouth. But she couldn't tell Ana that. "And I eat my pizza from the crust to the point."

Ana laughed, but not in a mean way. "Okay, that first one's pretty good, but how is the second one even a secret? As soon as we ate pizza together, I'd figure it out anyway."

The panic in Katie's chest eased, and she laughed along with Ana. When she looked at her friend, open-faced and smiling, the secrets she hadn't spoken coiled up and settled deep inside Katie. They were safer there. It was better this way. The little-bit-sick feeling in her stomach made Katie wonder if she was totally right, but she pushed that deeper inside too.

Some secrets, she thought, *I'm allowed to keep.*

That night, when her parents' bedroom had been dark and silent long enough that she could be sure they were asleep, Katie clicked on her small flashlight and headed for the attic.

In her old house, Katie had known exactly where the creaky spots in the floor were, but this house still felt unfamiliar sometimes. Twice she made a floorboard groan and held her breath afterward, as though that would suck up the sound.

When Katie had safely scaled the steps to the attic, she found the box waiting in a dusty pool of moonlight. The beautiful things inside pulled on her heart even more now, and somehow they seemed to be tugging at her memory too.

Katie wanted to keep them all close, but she decided to take only one thing at a time. That way, if her mom decided to check, she'd be less likely to notice something was missing. But which one should she take first?

It didn't take long to decide. It was the pocket watch Katie loved most. She held up the small circle and breathed in deeply, but the watch only smelled like old metal. Somehow, she'd been expecting it to smell like something else.

Like cloves.

Katie closed the box carefully and snuck down the attic stairs, but she wasn't quite ready to go back to bed. After listening at her parents' door to be sure they were still asleep, she made her way down the next flight of stairs, past the doorway draped with Thankfuls. She paused and touched her fingertips to the curls of paper, wondering what had made her write the secret words about her birth parents, worrying once again about what her mom and dad might think when they read that last link.

There was no mess left in the kitchen. The only signs

of all the hours Katie's mom had spent preparing the feast were the turkey brining in the sink and the shelf of pies in the fridge. The counters had been wiped spotless and the dishes and spices put away, including the cloves. But it was only a few moments before Katie had the small bottle clutched in one hand and the pocket watch in the other.

Back in her room and under her pile of quilts, Katie opened the spice bottle and set it on the closest corner of her nightstand, hoping it might help her remember more. She slid the pocket watch under the covers in case her mom checked on her in the night.

After that, it took Katie hours to fall asleep. Now she was keeping too many secrets, and she was beginning to realize how many her parents were keeping from her. A new worry began to grow inside her as she thought of the stories her parents had told her and wondered about the ones they hadn't.

Nothing felt like solid ground anymore. If you could become a family "just like that," was it real? And could it last forever?

Katie's mind flashed back to the night at the pond: the ice that had seemed safe, in spite of the dark, cold secrets of the water beneath. The shock when Ana had broken through and they'd all tumbled into the icy water, even though Katie had suspected all along it would happen.

How long until the ground gave way beneath her again?

Ana

Chapter 7

BABUSHKA DRAGGED MIKEY and Ana, drenched and
shivering, away from the pond and up the hillside. Ana
had never been so cold. The air seemed to be forming frost
inside her lungs.

"We're fine," she said, her teeth chattering like Mikey's
orange marbles. "My mom will take care of us." Ana didn't
even have to look at Babushka to know neither one of them

believed that. But wow, did she want to believe. It hurt to realize how much.

"Your mother," Babushka said, "has gone to bed. She is very tired because her life is very tiresome." She tipped her head toward Ana, like a crow on a fence post. "I take care of you now." Babushka could freeze even normal words into shards of ice.

In her room, Ana threw on dry clothes, then came back to help Mikey. But Babushka had beat her to him.

Mikey stood on the cold tile floor with his knobby knees trembling as Babushka ran the bathwater. He reminded Ana of the house on chicken legs from her dad's stories. Or maybe it was Babushka who had reminded her of the old witch who lived in that house.

"Now I tell you what happened next to Vasilisa, the girl who lost her parents." Babushka glanced up at Ana. "She was troublesome to her stepmother, so she was sent to the witch, Baba Yaga."

Ana shivered. Wasn't that the same witch she'd just remembered? One she hadn't thought about in years?

Babushka cracked open the window to let the steam out. The snow was coming down hard now, and a draft of wind curled around her, lifting the white wisps of her hair at the exact moment Ana realized that "Baba Yaga" sounded a lot like "Babushka."

"And do you know what the witch did with that girl?"

Ana rolled her eyes, trying not to be scared. "Cooked her in the oven?"

Babushka cackled. "Not this time. She had eaten plenty of children before, but Baba Yaga had something else in mind for Vasilisa." She pointed a bony finger at Mikey, then at the bathtub. He scrambled in.

"Do not drown while I am gone, Mikhail," Babushka ordered as she handed him a bar of soap. She took Ana by the arm and led her downstairs and out the front door. "I will tell you what the witch did with her troublesome girl," she said. "She put the girl to work."

Babushka thrust a snow shovel toward Ana. "It will be easier to shovel tomorrow if you move the first layer tonight. You are welcome."

"I'm not doing it unless my mom says so. She won't make me shovel." It was probably true, but Ana knew her Mom wouldn't exactly be shoveling either. They'd probably just stay snowed in until Ana gave in and took care of it, but that didn't mean she wanted to get started tonight.

"Your mother needs rest." Babushka tapped the shovel

against the ground. "I am in charge."

"I'm not doing it," Ana said. "I don't even have my coat."

Babushka took off her own coat and held it out, hooked over her fingers and smelling of onions and pain-relief rub.

"You are welcome again," she said as Ana put the coat on.

When Babushka had disappeared into the house, Ana slammed the shovel into the walk and began scraping. The snow was coming down hard, which she usually loved because she was usually watching it from somewhere warm.

Ana worked in a steady rhythm: *scrape, chuck, scrape, chuck.* When she slid a little and held the shovel in her hands, when the air cooled her lungs as the work warmed her body, it almost felt like hockey. The rhythm reminded her of drills during practice.

Slide, stop, slap shot.

Slide, stop, slap shot.

After she'd pushed the last line of snow from the driveway, Ana stopped and closed her eyes. She tipped her face upward and let the cold kisses of snowflakes cover her. Even though she'd never admit it to Babushka, it felt kind of good to have that gentle ache in her muscles again and the solid heartbeat in her chest. To feel the snowflakes on her face instead of watching them through a window.

Ana left the shovel on the porch and shucked Babushka's rough coat. She went to the fridge and grabbed the milk, and when she shut the door, there was Babushka, sitting at the counter and knitting some ugly red socks.

"Lucky you have a snow shovel. In Russia, we only had a coal shovel. Lucky you like being outside in the snow. You are a lucky, lucky girl, Anastasia Ilyinichna Petrova."

In her mind, Ana laid out all the unlucky cards she'd been dealt lately. Dad gone, Mom a mess, Mikey crying, and now Babushka running her life and reminding her of that whole ridiculous name. "Yeah. Super lucky."

"You will rest tonight, rebyonok," Babushka said, clicking the knitting needles. "You will need much energy to do all the housework waiting for you in the morning." The thin snake of yarn turned around itself and around the needles, again and again, even though Babushka's eyes were locked with Ana's. She could almost believe the needles and yarn were knitting on their own, more bewitched than simply moved by Babushka.

Later, when Babushka had gone to her room, Ana

crept out of bed to tell her mom everything that had gone wrong. But as she laid her hand on the doorknob, she realized she didn't know what to say. She never knew what to say. As bad as things were for her, she didn't want to make them worse for her mom.

So instead, Ana grabbed the puck and tiptoed toward Mikey's room. Maybe she could help her mom by helping Mikey. She couldn't let him go to bed thinking everybody had let him down.

Ana eased open Mikey's door and slipped through, but once she'd shut it behind her, she could barely see a thing.

"Hey," she whispered into the darkness. Ana thrust her hands in front of her and tried to feel for the softness of Mikey's quilt or the prickly fuzziness of his short hair. "Are you awake?"

Mikey clicked on a flashlight. "I thought you were her." He gave a little shudder.

"Why is it so dark in here?" Ana asked. She'd never had to feel her way around in Mikey's room before.

"She took my night-light," Mikey said, clutching the flashlight in one hand and the end of the paper countdown chain in the other. "She told me more of that story with the girl and the witch and the glowing skull heads. I told her I was scared, but she still took my night-light because she thinks I'm too old for it. But I'm not even old. *She's* old. And she keeps calling me Mikhail."

At least he seemed more mad than sad. At least he'd outsmarted Babushka with his flashlight.

Ana picked up a crayon from Mikey's floor and took the paper chain from him. She counted five links down and drew a little lightbulb. "This is the day she's leaving," she said. "Then you'll get your night-light back, so you can count down to that too."

As Mikey studied the new picture, Ana held out the hockey puck. "Try one more wish," she said. "The other stuff will work, just . . . try something else. Something small but important." *Sort of like you,* she thought.

Mikey scrunched his nose. "Why does magic have so many rules?"

Ana shook her head. "I don't know, but it'll be worth it. Come on. Small but important."

Mikey thought for a second, then grabbed the puck from Ana. He held it between his palms and whispered his wish. "Candy bar pie. I want candy bar pie for Thanksgiving, like our real grandma used to make us."

Of course, Babushka was technically their real

grandma too, but Ana knew what Mikey meant. As soon as he'd said the words, Ana could taste the pie herself, with just the right amount of chocolate and crunch under a snowbank of whipped cream.

"That does sound good, Mikey. That's perfect." Except thinking about Grandma Mary just reminded Ana of one more thing she'd lost. "I wish I'd let her teach me how to bake. Or at least paid attention when she did it herself."

Mikey patted Ana's hand. "It doesn't matter if we can't bake. That's what the magic is for."

Right. The magic.

Ana kissed the puck, which tasted *nothing* like candy bar pie, and whispered the spell.

Then she knew exactly what to do. Maybe she could make Mikey's wish come true after all.

The next morning, Ana waited until Babushka had dragged her mom down to the basement to sort through boxes. Then she stole the ugly red socks from Babushka's knitting bag and snuck out of the house. If there was one person in Boston who could bake candy bar pie just like Grandma Mary had, it was Katie's mom.

Mrs. Burton was in the kitchen, which was no surprise,

but she seemed to knead her dough extra hard after she saw Ana. "No more late night swims," she said. "I've got my eye on you, Ana Petrova. You keep my Katie safe."

Ana had always thought Katie's mom treated Katie like a kitten, too small and fragile to fend for herself. But now definitely wasn't the time to bring that up.

"Absolutely. Safety is my number-one priority. Um, Mrs. Burton, I have a favor to ask you."

Mrs. Burton gave Ana the suspicious side-eye look, but she turned curious instead when she saw the recipe card in Ana's hand.

"It's my grandma's recipe," Ana offered. "It would mean a lot if you could make it for me."

Mrs. Burton looked like she might be caving, but she shook her head. "The menu's set, and my time's spoken for this morning. I have my own pies to bake, and that turkey needs some attention." But she didn't hand the card back.

"Actually, it's not for me. It's for Mikey. He's had kind of a rough year. This was the one thing he wanted for Thanksgiving." Ana remembered something else that might help her cause. "And Katie hates pumpkin, so if you made a couple of these instead, we'd each have one."

The card bent a little in Mrs. Burton's grip. "Katie hates pumpkin pie?" She dropped to a stool. "She never tells me these things. Maybe she would like this better."

Ana decided this was close enough to a yes that she'd close the gap herself. "Oh, she totally would. You're the best mom ever. I'll pick ours up tomorrow. And I'll keep Katie busy the rest of the day so it can be a surprise!"

Before Mrs. Burton could argue, Katie herself showed up, and the deal was done. *Perfect,* thought Ana. *Finally, something went right.*

Thanksgiving Day at Ana's house was a Russian disaster, right from the very beginning.

"Today," announced Babushka as they sat around the table, eating runny oatmeal, "we call your father."

Mikey looked at Ana, who looked at her mom, who looked at the ceiling.

"No," Ana said. "No thanks."

"We call. Where is your phone?"

Ana scraped back from the table and pulled her mom's phone off the charger, where it had sat, 100% charged, for probably two weeks. She held it behind her back.

"We're not calling," she said. "He wouldn't answer

anyway. He used to, but not anymore. Not for months."

Babushka snorted. "My son will answer when I call."

Ana shook her head. "It's the same number even if you call. He probably blocked it or something."

"Let her try." Ana's mom still stared at the ceiling, and she didn't even brush away the tear that slid clear to her collar. "Let her find out for herself."

Ana shoved the phone into Babushka's outstretched hand and walked away. She sat on the stairs where she could still hear, folding her legs up and resting her forehead on her knees.

She wanted to be wrong. She wanted to hear Babushka barking at her dad in Russian, and for that to fix something, somehow.

He didn't answer. Of course.

Then everything was worse. Of course.

Babushka banned Ana from the kitchen and put her to work clearing out Mikey's room. Mikey was supposed to be helping, but all he did was bawl over every little thing she chucked. Ana tried to peek into the kitchen to see what all the strange, sour smells could be, but Babushka shooed her out over and over.

By the time Babushka called them to the table,

everybody was broken-down and exhausted. And then, Ana saw the food.

Babushka had ruined the turkey with a strange gray sauce they weren't allowed to scrape off. She'd axed the sweet potatoes.

"Mom," Ana pleaded. "Where is the real food?"

Babushka slapped her palm against the table. "Sugared cranberries on turkey? Marshmallows on yams? Your teeth will rot away like old stumps!"

Ana ran her tongue over her fillings. They hadn't come from Thanksgiving dinner. That was just dumb. And wouldn't it be worse to starve? Babushka's dinner wasn't even edible.

The potatoes were chunky instead of mashed and served with boiled radishes that tasted like barf. The rolls were crusty and flecked with something black, but Ana and Mikey still ate three each until Babushka took the basket. After that, they had to settle for their mom's sad, limp asparagus.

"Ana," Mikey begged as they helped clear the table after it was finally over. "I'm still hungry."

Babushka appeared in the doorway. Hadn't she been all the way over at the sink half a second ago?

"I heard this! What child is hungry when he carries a bowl of radishes?" Babushka dragged Mikey back to his chair. "Starving children in Russia can only imagine such a feast."

Babushka whipped a dirty wooden spoon from her apron, longer than any Ana had seen in their kitchen before. She dipped the spoon into the bowl and tipped out the contents: three fat radishes dropped like greasy stones onto Mikey's plate.

"Eat all three," she said, "before you leave the chair." She towered over him, clutching her wooden spoon like a club.

Mikey's chin quivered.

"You can do it," Ana whispered.

Mikey nodded and speared the smallest radish. He popped it in his mouth and smashed his eyes shut, then started chewing rabbit-fast. After a few seconds, though, his eyes popped open, and he gagged a little.

"Just swallow it," Ana said. "And take a drink. Quick!"

Mikey nodded again. He tried to swallow, twice, but both times he ended up choking and spluttering. "Go, Mikey, go!" Ana chanted. Mikey gripped his fork and swallowed, and this time, the radish went down.

For a second.

Mikey had barely enough time to reach for his water and bring the glass to his lips before the radish came back up and out. Little red chunks swirled in the water and settled on the bottom of the glass.

"Revolting," Babushka declared, waving the spoon at Mikey's regurgitated radish soup. For the first time maybe ever, Ana and Mikey both agreed with her. Ana peeked over at Babushka. Even the old witch had to give Mikey credit for trying, right?

Wrong. Babushka pointed the wooden spoon at the other two radishes. "Those two must stay down."

"Mom!" Ana called. No mother should stand by while her kid got tortured like this, no matter what kind of day she was having.

Ana's mom appeared from the kitchen. "What?" she asked, like that one word was exhausting. "What do you need?" Like anything they answered would be way too much.

"She's force-feeding Mikey!" Ana cried. "You've got to fix this."

"Okay," she said. She took a step backward and pressed her fingertips to her forehead.

It's not okay, Ana thought. *You can't shut down right now. You've got to do something.*

After a long silence, Ana's mom finally spoke. "Okay. Babushka, could you help with dessert?" She shuffled back into the kitchen with Babushka close behind, clucking instructions at her.

As soon as they'd disappeared again, Ana set down the bowl she'd been carrying on the closest counter. She peeked into the kitchen, where her mom and Babushka seemed to be talking pretty seriously. They were only in the next room, but Ana had never missed her mother so much.

No. Feeling sorry for herself wouldn't get them anywhere. Babushka was busy, so it was time.

"Okay, Mikey," Ana whispered. "Close your eyes."

Mikey let his eyelids close, which pushed two round tears down his cheeks.

"What about the radishes?" he asked. "I can't eat them. Don't make me do it. Is this a trick?"

"Don't worry about the radishes. Think about your pie wish, as hard as you can. And don't open your eyes until I tell you."

Ana grabbed the slimy radishes from Mikey's plate

and dashed out the back door. She tossed them over the fence and into the darkness, then hurried to where she'd been chilling Mrs. Burton's perfect candy bar pie on top of a pile of snow. She tried to plan out the best way to get a pie slicer and a plate without Babushka noticing, but then she had a much better idea.

Ana crept back to the dining room and traded Mikey's dinner plate for the whole pie, with its golden, flaky crust and gentle waves of whipped cream.

"Open your eyes."

Mikey's eyes popped open and bugged right out. "Thank you thank you thank you," he said. And right before Ana said "You're welcome," he looked up toward heaven (or at least Ana's bedroom) and added, "I owe you one, magic hockey puck."

Ana was okay with the fact that the puck had gotten all the credit. Especially when Babushka came in with a cold raisin pudding jiggling in one hand and a Jell-O salad with trapped celery curls quivering in the other.

"Oh, don't those look scrumptious?" Ana asked, before Babushka could say a word. "I think Mikey's all set, so let's dig in! Hey, is that celery in there?"

"Hay is for mules," Babushka growled. She narrowed

her eyes as she scooped one shivering glop of pudding into a bowl and dropped it in front of Ana.

Ana knew she'd won, even though Babushka's pudding tasted like salty gray mud with raisin slugs. The smile on Mikey's face as he ate his candy bar pie still made it feel, just for a second, like the best Thanksgiving ever.

His smile, and the huge piece of pie Ana snuck after everybody else had gone to bed.

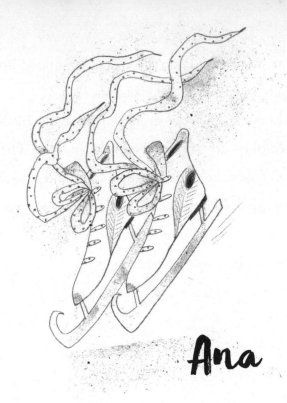

Ana

Chapter 8

THE CANDY BAR pie was long gone by Sunday, but Ana took great satisfaction from knowing that Babushka would soon be long gone too. That morning, she woke up extra early to get the laundry done so Babushka could start packing. No way was she going to let anything mess up this departure. Ana wanted Babushka gone so bad she was willing to touch her dirty underwear.

With a basket of fresh clothes against her hip, Ana

returned to her room to fold. She dumped the laundry onto her bed and grabbed an armful, letting herself relax for one second while everything was still warm and clean.

"Hey, Ana!"

Ana yelped. Some people had monsters under their beds. Ana just had a little brother, but sometimes that was even scarier.

"Mikey. Do *not* sneak into my room. You're going to give me a heart attack. And hay is for mules." Ana clamped her hand over her mouth. Had she just quoted Babushka? Should she wash her mouth out with soap or something?

Mikey scrambled out and pulled the puck from under his shirt. "I'm ready to make my next wish."

Oh, geez. Ana was half tempted to tell Mikey the real story behind the candy bar pie, but she couldn't do it when he'd finally started to believe.

She shoved the laundry over and sat next to Mikey. "Let's hear what you've got."

Mikey closed his eyes and whispered to the puck. "If I can't wish for Dad to come back, I wish Markov could live here instead of Babushka."

Markov. Two years ago, he'd lived with Ana's family during his rookie season. At first, Ana hadn't been sure about the brand-new Bruin their dad had brought home, and neither had her mom. He was just so huge and hard to understand. But Mikey had known right away what a good guy he was. Ana smiled at the memory.

Mikey giggled. "Remember when I taught him how to play hide-and-seek and he got stuck under his bed?"

"Remember when he came to my hockey games and had to sit in the back because he got so worked up?"

Ana realized that she'd been worried about Mikey's crying for so long she'd almost forgotten how much she loved his little laugh, straight up from his belly, true as could be. For a second, she almost believed in the magic herself.

Then Mikey lowered his voice to a whisper. "Remember when he sneezed on mom's lasagna and he felt so bad he made a new dinner?"

Ana could almost taste Markov's dinner then, even though she could only remember that it was warm and creamy and a tiny bit spicy. "Remember how his cooking actually tasted good?"

Then other memories flashed into Ana's mind. She felt herself skating beside Markov as he told her how he'd learned to play hockey on a frozen pond in one of the poorest parts of Moscow. The game had saved him, and he'd wanted to do that for other kids. That's why he'd helped her so much, Ana knew, and why he'd started Bruins Giving Back.

Every home game, the Bruins gave away tickets and BGB jerseys to kids from after-school youth programs. The kids got to watch the game and go into the VIP area to high-five the Bruins in the tunnel at the beginning of the third period. The whole thing had been Markov's idea, but Ana's mom had helped make it happen—which was why there was still a box of BGB jerseys in their basement.

"Markov was the best," Mikey said. Ana agreed, but it wasn't just that. He made them be their best too. Made her mom part of big projects, made her dad want to be at Ana's games, made Ana want to practice and really improve. And for one whole season, he'd slept right in the bedroom where Babushka was staying now.

Ana remembered Mikey's wish. "It would be awesome to have him back," she said. "But remember, our wishes can't control anybody else. Keep thinking, okay buddy?"

Mikey nodded. "Yeah. Okay." He let the puck fall from his fingers and walked away without another word.

The puck had let him down again. No, *Ana* had let

him down again. She had to figure something out.

Ana went to her closet and pulled out the big Bruins poster from that two-years-ago team when Markov was a rookie. As she unrolled it, she remembered her dad's strong, scarred hands spreading it out in the locker room for everybody to sign. The Bruins had clinched the division that night, but he'd still told everyone how Ana's team had won their division too. How she was the top scorer on her team.

Had he thought of her when he'd stood for team pictures with the Flyers this year?

Nobody else could have read the signatures on the poster, but Ana still knew every one, and suddenly the Bruins felt like another family she'd lost.

The Bruins had been good two years ago because they were strong in every position. Consistent goalie. Tough defense. Strong, slippery scorers. The same thing had been true of her own team last year. Take away any of those pieces and they wouldn't have won a single game. How many times had her coach said it?

Then Ana knew.

She couldn't believe she hadn't seen it before.

The reason her family couldn't seem to win, or even

stay in the game, was that they were missing one of the most important positions. How were you supposed to be a family with an empty spot in the roster?

She had to get her dad back. She *had* to.

So what if he hadn't answered when they'd called on Thanksgiving? He hadn't known Ana was there too. He'd probably thought it was her mom and they'd start fighting. He probably didn't know there wasn't any fight left in her anymore.

So what if he thought he belonged in Philadelphia? He'd just forgotten how good things could be in Boston. He was always saying what a terrible memory he had from getting hit so much on the ice. Maybe it had gotten worse, but she could help him remember. She could do so much better than she'd ever done before.

Ana grabbed her tablet and looked up the Flyers' schedule. Maybe they were coming to town and she could score some tickets. Maybe going to a game would ease some of her own ache from missing hockey so much.

Then Ana saw something even better:

Flyers versus Bruins in the Winter Classic. Her dad would be facing off against his old team right there in Boston in the best game of the season.

Once a year, two NHL teams battled it out in an outdoor game at New Year's. Seeing the players under the big blue sky always felt so right, like the game was pure again. Like pond hockey between kids, even if the kids had million-dollar contracts and were playing in a billion-dollar stadium.

And this year it was happening in Boston. Ana could help her dad remember right here—a fresh start on New Year's Day during his favorite game of all.

Plus, it gave her some time to plan things out. Ana wasn't the world's best planner, and she couldn't risk this ending up as badly as her first attempt at ice-skating this season. Better to get it right than to rush. And definitely better to do it after Babushka was gone. Best of all to do it at the Winter Classic.

Ana kept plotting and planning as she folded, then gathered all Babushka's clothes into a basket and delivered them to the corner of the guest room. She grabbed the old suitcase and swung it up onto Babushka's bed. Time to get the witch on her way. But when she unzipped the suitcase and swung the lid open, there, shining up at her, was a fancy silver pocket watch, looking totally out of place.

Babushka hated anything fancy or pretty.

"What the heck is that?" she asked, not expecting an answer.

"My property," said Babushka.

Ana whipped around. "Hey," she said, trying to act natural. "Do you want me to help you pack?"

"I have told you, hay is for mules," Babushka grumbled. "Not children. Not even wild ones."

Babushka shut the suitcase and swept it out of sight. "This watch is no business of yours. And there is no packing because there is no leaving." She jammed the suitcase back under the bed. "When you finish the wash, look for my new red socks. They disappeared from my knitting bag."

"You're not leaving?" Ana felt her eyes bugging out. "Does my mom know?"

"This was her idea," said Babushka, calmly putting all her clean laundry into the drawers instead of into the suitcase.

Ana raced down the hall and burst into her mom's room. This time, she knew exactly what she wanted to say.

"She's not leaving?"

"Ana," said her mom, looking somewhere over Ana's shoulder. "How would you feel if Babushka stayed with us for a while?"

Ana had been tiptoeing around her mom too long, and this was too much. "Do you mean 'How would I feel?' or 'Here's the deal'? It sure sounds like you already decided."

Ana's mom fidgeted with the edge of her sleeve. "We've only been talking about it the last couple of days, but it's been so nice having another adult around to help."

There were about six thousand words Ana would've used to describe Babushka's visit before she picked "nice." And didn't all the work Ana had been doing the last four months count for anything?

"Are you serious? How long?"

"Until winter break, maybe. I'm going to start working from home again, part-time."

Ana stared. "I thought that was what you'd been doing all year."

Her mom looked away. "I took a leave of absence, but I'm going back."

Ana couldn't believe she was about to receive the ultimate Babushka punishment because her mom had been slacking. But then her mom stood in front of her and rested her hands on Ana's shoulders, and Ana could see the tired in her eyes.

"I promise you, this will help us get back to normal."

Normal. That was the whole point of the plan—to get their family back to normal. She had to admit that Babushka had helped a little.

The house didn't look like a tornado zone so much anymore. Some of the Russian food actually tasted okay now. And most of all, Babushka had started taking Ana's mom on long walks around the neighborhood, even in the snow. Ana could barely believe it, since her mom hadn't been going anywhere lately and she wasn't really related to Babushka. Babushka was just the mom of the guy who'd broken her heart.

Ana did a quick calculation in her head. Winter break was twenty-seven days away. It would be terrible, but she'd survive, if this was what it would take to get their normal family back.

"Until winter break—or maybe less, if we don't need her anymore?"

"Until winter break, or maybe until the end of the school year."

Ana didn't even try to count how many days were left

until the end of the school year. She didn't need to—it was way past the deadline. Past the Winter Classic. What if Babushka tried to stick around even after her son came back? No way was Ana piecing her family back together with Babushka still part of it.

"She can stay until New Year's," Ana said. "But that's it. I'll start the countdown. New Year, new us. That's my final offer."

Ana couldn't look at her mom or she'd cave. Getting upset was as easy as jumping off the diving board, but it was never long before Ana splashed down and cooled right off. How did people *stay* mad? It was a mystery. Ana hadn't even been able to stay mad at her dad.

"Okay," said her mom, and she tried to smile. "I'll do my best."

Ana wanted to hug her, but she didn't. If she didn't learn to stay mad, nobody would ever take her seriously. If she didn't stick to her plan, Babushka would be here forever, and she'd never get things back to normal. Instead, she just nodded, then walked away with her arms pressed to her sides.

That night, Ana heard sniffling and sobbing coming from Mikey's room.

He was crying.

Again.

Babushka had undone all Ana's hard work, all her *magic*, and tomorrow Mikey would have to go back to school in worse shape than ever. She crept out of bed and paused at his door, where not even a hint of light glowed in the crack underneath.

So the witch still had his night-light. At least Ana could do something about that, even if she'd already gotten in trouble once today for snooping.

Ana steeled herself as she stole into Babushka's room and rifled through her dresser. The old pocket watch gave a faint *chik-chok*, and Ana half expected to find it every time she opened a drawer. But she found Mikey's Zamboni night-light first.

As Ana creaked Mikey's door open, he swooshed the covers over his head. "Mikey," she whispered between his wails. "It's me."

Mikey peeked out. "Oh good," he said, giving one last little shuddering sob. "It's even darker tonight."

"Not for long," Ana said.

"I thought she was leaving." His little voice wavered through the darkness. A soft *chik-chik* told Ana he had the marbles in his hands. "I thought I'd get my night-light back, but Mom says Babushka is staying."

"Yeah, but that doesn't mean you can't have your night-light back." She plugged it in, and Mikey's face lit up as she sat at the edge of his bed.

"We can't control her, kiddo," Ana said. "She has her own magic that's even stronger than ours. But we can still win. You know why?"

Mikey shrugged.

"Because there are two of us. Things are always better in pairs." She took his hands and tapped the lucky marbles together. "You're the one who taught me that." With her thumbs, Ana wiped Mikey's cheeks dry. "But we have to be brave."

"Pairs are better," Mikey agreed. "I can be brave."

"It won't be that much longer," she said. She went to Mikey's messy desk and clicked on the lamp. "Do you have paper?" she asked. "And scissors and a glue stick?"

Together, they cut ten new links and attached them to the end of Mikey's chain.

"There," Ana said. "By the time we get to the end of this, your first wish will have come true. You'll be having happy days again."

The stairs creaked, and Ana and Mikey froze as the spooky melody of Babushka's humming floated down the hall. Her bedroom door shut with a whine and a click, and Ana crossed her fingers, hoping she'd put everything back in exactly the right place.

After a few minutes, Ana figured they were safe. But still, she kissed Mikey's little head and stayed by him until his breathing grew slow and even, hoping that before Mikey's chain ran out, she'd get everything back in the right place for her family too.

Katie

Chapter 9

WITH LESS THAN a month of links left on her Thankful Chain, Katie had started working on making the perfect presents for the people she loved. She threaded beads onto a thin, silver wire to the *chik-chok* of the pocket watch.

There was something so reassuring about having everything in neat patterns, just where it belonged. Heart, space, jewel, space. Heart, space, jewel, space. Only a few to go before she could start on the second half of the bracelet for Ana's Hanukkah present. Then she could work on her parents' presents, once she figured out what to make for them. Everything had to be perfect this year.

The gentle rhythm of the pocket watch helped keep Katie's hands in a steady rhythm. She had kept the watch near her for eight straight nights, and she'd kept the box of cloves too. The rest of the house smelled of the giant fir tree in the family room, which Katie loved. But when she needed it, she could smell this almost-memory of her old life too.

Tonight, though, her family would gather around that tree and read another Thankful from their chains, which meant they'd be one link closer to the Thankful she'd written about her birth parents. As she crimped another bead into just the right spot on the wire, Katie tried to picture that moment. But no matter how many times she tried, she couldn't imagine anything but hurting the parents she loved and deepening the divide between them. Should she sneak down and change what she'd written? Get rid of that link altogether?

Links, Katie thought as she attached a tiny fastener to the bracelet. That was the problem. Katie felt outside it all. Everyone seemed to be neatly connected but her, and even the perfect presents couldn't fix that. She wrote the words from Grace's letters on a small scrap of paper, wanting to believe them.

Remember this truth: you are not alone.

Then, like a sign, a single light shone from Ana's window. *See if you can come over.* Katie strained to see her friend behind the light, but the room seemed empty. It was hard to tell, though, with the sun slanting toward her.

Still, there was no mistaking the signal. Maybe today would be the day she'd finally have the courage to tell Ana all her secrets.

Katie fixed the last fastener onto the bracelet and brushed the rest of the jewelry supplies into their bin. The second half of the bracelet would be easier now that she'd figured out how to make the first.

"Mom," she asked as she hurried down the stairs, "can I go over to Ana's house?"

Katie's mom sat at the center of a room littered with Christmas decorations. "Will you help me for a few minutes first? It's no fun by myself, and we need to get this done today so we can go to your appointment tomorrow."

How was it that the things you were dreading could creep up on you like that? Even though they'd been waiting months to see Katie's new cardiologist, it didn't seem possible that those months had passed so quickly.

"I guess I can help for a little while," Katie said. Ana would understand. She wasn't the most patient, but she never stayed mad, and they'd still have time to hang out. Plus, she might have distracted herself with something else already.

Together, Katie and her mom wound small white lights around the fresh pine boughs on the mantel. Katie carefully placed thick candles between the branches, wondering why she'd never noticed they looked almost like the trunks of upside-down trees growing into the woodwork. Everything looked just like it always had, just like it was supposed to. But somehow, none of it seemed quite right anymore.

"See if this looks good up there too, will you?" her mom asked. "I'm not sure where to put it in this new house."

Katie caught her breath when her mom handed her a round red nesting doll just like the one she'd seen in the box.

Well, almost. This one was bigger and seemed different

somehow, like it had been painted by a machine instead of a person. It still looked like a mother, but a too-perfect mother with bright red lips and brown waves of hair beneath her shawl. And there were no initial-like letters painted on the bottom.

"I don't remember this," she said. "Where did we put it in the old house?"

"On top of the bookshelf," her mom said. "You may not have been tall enough to notice it." She cracked open the first figurine. "There's another one inside," she said. "And another one inside that."

"I know," Katie said. She got the feeling somehow that she'd always known, even before she'd found the box in the attic. But maybe she wasn't supposed to.

Katie's mom handed the pieces to her. "They're called nesting dolls, but they have other names too. Matryoshka dolls. Some Americans call them babushka dolls. My mother gave me these when I was little, and someday I'll give them to you."

Katie tried to feel grateful, but the matryoshka dolls she really wanted were the ones in the attic.

"On the mantel?" she asked. "In front of the branches?" When her mom nodded, Katie cracked open the rest of the figures, then fit the halves back together and lined them up.

Each one next to her mother, she thought. Katie had never met her grandma, the one who had given her mother these dolls and so many of her recipes. They'd been alive at the same time, just for a year, but that was before Katie had been adopted. She touched the little dolls one by one, starting with the tallest, and her eyes studied each, searching for some little imperfection.

It wasn't until she reached the smallest one that she saw something: an extra stroke, almost like a mistake, on both of the eyes. It made the doll seem sad, and different from the others. Katie scooted it a little farther away. Not far enough her mom would notice and fix it. For some reason, Katie didn't want this to be fixed.

"Okay," she said. "I'm done. Can I go to Ana's house now?"

Katie's mom nodded. "You two come back here if you want. Mikey is always welcome too, you know."

"I know, Mom. And it's okay if we go to Ana's house once in a while."

Katie stepped out her back door and squinted in the bright afternoon light. The pond still shone frosty blue as she passed, even though the snow didn't seem nearly so magical now that it was dirty and she'd been trudging through it for over a week. Footprints clumped and trailed all around the shore, but none of them went all the way to the ice.

So nobody was skating yet. How long before they could try again? Long enough for her mom to forget about the last time?

Ana would know. Katie pulled one hand from its mitten to knock on her best friend's front door.

But when the door swung open, Katie gasped and stepped back to make sure she didn't have the wrong house.

It was the old lady from the pond.

The one Ana had sworn was in Katie's imagination.

Thin pieces of hair, white as fresh snow, had escaped the old woman's bun. As she wrapped her shawl around herself and bent to study Katie's face, Katie wondered if she'd somehow stepped into a storybook. An old woman in a shawl! And the rose pattern of the fabric—it reminded her of the nesting dolls.

Before she could gather the courage to speak, Ana grabbed Katie by the arm and hurried her inside and toward the stairs. "What are you doing here?" she whispered.

"I'm your best friend. What's *she* doing here? The lady who supposedly doesn't exist?"

Ana hesitated half a second, then waved a hand toward the woman, who still watched them from the doorway. "Oh, *that* old lady. I didn't know you were talking about her." Ana's laugh sounded false and forced. "That's just my grandma. She's a little different."

"Babushka!" the woman said. "Babushka! Babushka!"

"See what I mean?" asked Ana.

Babushka? Katie wondered. *Like the dolls?*

Katie tried to get another peek, but Ana dragged her to the kitchen, where Mikey sat on a bar stool, pairing up forks and spoons.

"Hi, Katie," he said. "Did you run here or something?"

Katie hadn't even noticed she was still a little out of breath, or that there were beads of sweat along her hairline.

So here it was. The perfect chance to tell them about her heart problem, which would lead right into telling about her adoption. All Katie's secrets would be out.

But she couldn't quite do it. Not yet.

"Yeah," Katie lied. "I ran the whole way. I felt bad that I couldn't come right when you signaled."

"I didn't signal," Ana said.

Mikey tried to hide a laugh.

"Mikey, did you put a candle in my window?"

He broke into a full belly laugh, and Katie and Ana couldn't be mad. Maybe it was okay to have one more person in on the secret.

Ana rubbed her hands together. "Hey, did you hear about the field trip?"

Katie shook her head. "What field trip?"

"To my favorite skating rink in the universe."

"Seriously?" Katie asked. "And everybody gets to go?"

"All the fifth graders," Ana said, and Mikey gave a disappointed little moan. "As long as they've got all their homework turned in." Before Katie could even let this sink in, Ana leaned over and spoke in a sneaky whisper. "Now that you know about my grandma, want to see something cool?"

The last time Ana had asked Katie if she wanted to see something cool, they'd ended up setting Mrs. Clark's tarantula loose by accident. But still, Katie let Ana lead her upstairs and into an unfamiliar bedroom, where she pulled an old, brown suitcase from under the bed.

"Is this your grandma's?" Katie asked. "I don't know if we should be in here."

"Babushka will freak if she catches us, but this will only take a second. Check this out."

Ana popped the suitcase open, and Katie's heart raced.

A pocket watch, almost exactly like the one in her bed. Katie leaned closer, wondering if it was hers.

No. There was no scratch near the clasp. But otherwise, they were identical.

"Oh my goodness."

Ana reached toward the chain. "Doesn't it seem like pirate treasure or something? Will you give me five bucks if I take it?"

"It's not yours," Katie said. She tried to ignore the voice inside her pleading, *It's mine, it's mine*—even though she knew it wasn't.

"Looking for something?" Babushka appeared beside them, gripping a broomstick.

"No," Katie said. "We're sorry. We just . . ."

". . . just wanted to make sure I didn't drop any of your laundry in here last week." Ana slammed the suitcase shut and slid it back under the bed.

"Curious girls, hmm?" Babushka said. She came forward, shaking a gnarled finger at them. "The more you know, the sooner you grow old."

Katie shivered. That was almost exactly what her mom always said. Katie had to agree that Babushka did seem different, but maybe that was why she felt drawn to her. She wanted to ask Babushka about the strange saying, the pocket watch, and the rose-patterned shawl.

Babushka reached up and touched Katie's hair, and a warm sort of chill ran through her. "Ana," said Babushka. "This girl can teach you how to fix your hair. Then you will not look like a beggar."

Katie felt her face flush. It felt good to have Babushka's approval, but she didn't want it at Ana's expense.

"Oh, I didn't . . ."

Something crashed and shattered in the kitchen.

"Ack! Mikhail!"

Babushka rushed out of the room.

"I'd better get down there too so Mikey doesn't bawl," Ana said. "Just hang out here for a second."

Katie stood in the hallway, feeling absolutely awkward. Should she go to Ana's room? Go downstairs? Go home? A door creaked open.

"Ana?" called a weak voice.

"Just me," Katie said. "I'm sorry."

Ana's mom wrapped a robe tight around her and stepped into the hallway. "Katie. Hi. I didn't know you were coming over."

Katie searched for the right words to explain why she was standing there alone. "Well, there was just one candle in the window, so . . ." A warm flush crept into her cheeks. "That probably didn't make any sense." Why couldn't she just fit in and feel like family, like Ana had at her house? Why did Katie always feel like she didn't quite belong, no matter where she went?

"It's okay," Ana's mom said. "Do you know what made that crash?"

"Mikey," Katie said. "But Ana's down there, and so is her grandma."

"Oh," she said. "They don't need me, then." But she didn't sound relieved at all. She sounded every bit as unconnected as Katie felt, and as she turned to go, Katie struggled for the right words. When she slipped her hands in her pockets, she found them.

"Wait," she said. Ana's mom turned, and Katie stepped forward to press the paper into her hand.

Ana's mom unfolded the paper and whispered the words as she read them.

"Remember this truth: you are not alone." She wiped her eyes with the back of her hand. Finally, she looked up.

"Thank you," she said. "I hope you're right." She pulled Katie into her arms, and Katie could only think how different it felt from being hugged by her mother, how barely-there.

But before Katie could even hug her back, she was gone, and the door latched tight between them.

Ana

Chapter 10

ANA ALMOST BACKED down the stairs. Did she want to undo what had happened, or just un-see it?

Her mom had gotten out of bed, even though it was a bad day.

She'd been talking.

She'd hugged somebody.

Those were all good things. So why did Ana feel like she'd taken a puck to the chest?

Katie saw Ana and smiled. There was no backing away now. They stood there for a second, and that was all it took for Babushka to find them.

"Why are children today so idle?" she asked. "You are like a pair of crows. Standing around, poking at shiny things that do not belong to you. You need purpose." She crooked one finger toward herself, and both girls followed her into her room.

"Since you are so interested," she said, pulling out the suitcase, "and since you need purpose, I tell you about this." She took the pocket watch from the suitcase and thrust it toward them, pointing a gnarled finger at the bird on the back.

"Okay," said Ana. "But tell us the quick version."

Babushka huffed. "This is the firebird. And this," she said, pointing to a feather that wasn't quite connected to its tail, "is magic. Is purpose. If you have the feather of a firebird, a great quest has found you. You must return the feather to find your destiny, to make all your dreams come true. It is never easy, and it almost never works. It is a lonely and dangerous task. But you must try."

Ana tried not to roll her eyes. "So you're saying we should look for a feather?"

Babushka closed her hand and pulled the watch away. "The feather finds you. You must only recognize it and return it."

Ana flashed Babushka a thumbs-up. "Got it. Great advice. Thanks. We'll keep our eyes out for firebird feathers." She grabbed Katie by the elbow and started for the door. "Come on. We can check in my room first."

But when they got to Ana's room and flopped onto the bed, her elbow hit something hard. *Stupid puck.* Ana pulled it out from under the blankets, but she nearly dropped it again when she saw what was on it. She held it up to Katie.

"What does that look like?"

Katie squinted. "A hockey puck."

Ana held the puck even closer. "Okay, yeah, but what's on the puck?" She pointed to the Red Wings logo.

"Oh my gosh," Katie said. "It's a feather."

Ana dropped the puck like it had suddenly turned red hot. "I never thought of it as a quest, I guess, but ever since I showed Mikey this puck, it's like I've known there was something big I had to do."

Katie's eyes widened. "Like what?"

"She said you have to take the feather back to its owner, right? That's what I was thinking I needed to do anyway.

Well, not take the puck, but I need to find my dad. I need to bring him back."

Katie shifted on the bed, and something underneath squeaked.

"How are you going to do that?"

So Ana told Katie the whole win-Dad-back-at-the-Winter-Classic plan. Katie didn't look so sure.

"What?" Ana asked. "You don't think it will work, or you just don't think I can do it?"

"I don't know. It kind of seems dangerous. And I've never met your dad, but you said he hasn't ever come back to see you guys, so . . ."

Ana tried to pad herself against that blow. "So I should give up. Just sit here and do nothing. That's the answer? No wonder you and my mom are suddenly best friends."

Ana wished she could take that back when she saw the hurt on Katie's face.

"I don't do nothing," Katie said. "I just don't think you should go by yourself. Your mom would probably take you. Or Babushka could."

"Babushka couldn't, my mom wouldn't. Plus, it's not their quest and it's not their feather." She held up her hands in defense. "Not that I believe in that stuff! But still. It has to be me."

"And me!"

Mikey rolled out from under the bed.

"Oh, shoot. Mikey, you can't tell."

Mikey raised his eyebrows. "I won't tell if I can come."

Ana was stuck. Mikey might be good for convincing her dad to come home, but he also might slow her down. Still, there was only one answer that would keep him from yapping.

"Okay, you can come. See, Katie? I won't go by myself!"

Katie frowned. "That's not what I meant. Promise me you guys won't go alone. You could get lost. Or kidnapped." Mikey curled up like a kitten next to Katie, but Ana was too fired up to even sit down.

"Well, now you're acting just like *your* mom. Seriously, you've got to get a little courage!"

Katie looked away. "There's a difference between courage and crazy."

Ana threw her hands up. "There's also a difference between staying safe and not even living. You don't have to follow all the rules all the time."

"I kind of do," Katie said. She closed in on herself then,

like a flower. "But I don't expect you to understand why."

They were both silent for a minute. Finally, Katie smoothed Mikey's hair and stood up. "I'd better go home."

"Okay," Ana said. "See you tomorrow?"

Katie paused in the doorway. "At school, I guess. But you can't come over after. I have to . . . go somewhere."

What a fake excuse for a best friend to come up with. Ana could think of plenty of wrong things to say right then, but for once, she was smart enough not to say them.

Mikey scrambled up and grabbed Katie's hand, and she smiled down at him.

"Would you like to walk me home?" she asked.

Mikey nodded, and they disappeared together without even looking back. All that work, and now her best friend had stolen her little brother away, at least for now. Ana pictured them out on the sidewalk—Mikey chattering, Katie listening and nodding and saying just the right words until he hugged her too. All those months she had spent helping her mom, and Katie was the one she hugged.

For the first time all day, Ana felt cracks in her confidence. How was she ever supposed to put her family back together, when even her best friend found new ways to break them apart?

Chapter 11

KATIE WALKED TO school early the next morning, dodging every crack in the crumbly brick sidewalk. She'd wanted to walk alone because she wasn't sure what to say to Ana, but that ended up making things awkward all day. As the final bell approached, Katie hoped something could bring them back together before it was time to walk home.

When Ms. Decker started handing out permission

slips, Katie tried to give Ana a smile, but she seemed lost in her own world.

"This field trip is about coming together as one big fifth-grade family," Ms. Decker said. "And okay, it's about rewarding you for all your hard work too." She nodded at the new poster at the front of the class. "See where hard work can get you, folks? That's what I love about the Olympics."

The poster showed Elena Korsikova, the beautiful Russian skating star with the quadruple toe loop. Somehow she looked impossibly strong and incredibly graceful all at once. The Olympics were only a few weeks away, and Elena was suddenly everywhere.

Katie had spent the first ten years of her life without once wanting to skate, but the idea had been growing in her mind ever since the pond. She couldn't stop imagining herself gliding across the ice, carving graceful, lazy curves. Finally moving fast enough on her own two feet to feel the wind in her hair, even with her fragile heart.

If she could just get on the ice, it wouldn't matter that she was small—so was Elena Korsikova. It wouldn't matter that she'd had to leave her birth parents. Hadn't Elena Korsikova done the same thing when she left her family to train for the Olympics? Wouldn't she leave them an ocean behind when it was time to go for the gold?

Ms. Decker paused to make sure everybody was listening. "You've got two weeks, folks. If you have any assignments missing or forget your permission slip, you'll have to stay behind with Mrs. Truman in the library."

Katie loved Mrs. Truman, and she'd loved libraries ever since her afternoons with Grace back in Salt Lake. But this was *ice-skating*. She had to get her mom to sign the permission slip. That seemed like an Olympic-size feat on a day like today, though, when her mom would already be stressed about the appointment with Katie's new cardiologist.

After school, Katie found Ana and Mikey waiting outside, even though she'd said they couldn't come over. Even though everything had ended so awkwardly the day before.

"Hey," Katie said.

"Hey." Before any of them could figure out what to say next, Katie's car pulled into the pick-up circle.

"Oh," Ana said. "You really do have to go somewhere."

She seemed relieved, but Katie wasn't. Did her best friend think she was a liar?

Katie's mom rolled down her window. "Hop in, honey," she urged. "Ana, you're welcome to go grab a snack at our house, but we've got to get downtown."

Ana smiled at Katie, like everything was smoothed out between them already. "Sounds fun. Hey, Katie's got a permission slip for you to sign."

No, no, no. Stop talking.

But Ana didn't get the message. "Skating will be much safer this time, Mrs. Burton. I promise."

Katie jumped into the car and swung the door shut before Ana could say another word. She cringed, hoping her mom hadn't heard.

But she had. As they buckled up and pulled away, Katie's mom asked, "What's this about skating?" She checked the mirrors, even though Katie's dad was driving. "Ana doesn't think *you're* going ice-skating, does she?"

"Couldn't I?" Katie asked. "Carefully? It's a school trip. The whole fifth grade is going."

"I don't see why not," said Katie's dad. She wanted to hug him.

"Let's not get ahead of ourselves," said Katie's mom. "You'd be so vulnerable out on the ice with all those other kids. But I suppose it all depends on how things go today with Dr. Samha."

It all depends. Katie watched the city pass by her window. She'd gotten used to heart checkups with her old doctor in the hospital on the hillside. But what if this new doctor found new things wrong with her? What if her mom had been right about her heart all along? Katie still got out of breath so easily. Even now, she could feel her pulse quickening.

With every mile, her mom's words sank into Katie's skin and snaked through her veins.

It all depends on today.

Whether I can skate.

Whether I can keep pretending to be normal.

Whether I can start actually being *normal.*

Katie looked at her parents sitting in front of her and realized what it meant that they were both there. That her dad had stopped grading his final exams to drive them. That her mom was letting him drive, which only happened when she was fast asleep or too nervous. They were anxious about this too.

It all depends, she thought as they sped down the

parkway, past bicycles and buses and T trains full of people with the same healthy hearts they were born with. They had no idea how lucky they were.

It all depends.

Dr. Samha was about ten years older than the picture they'd seen online, but he was still younger than Katie's parents. He wore scrubs with alligators on them and perfectly round glasses. "Now then, young lady," he said. "What brings you here today? Chicken in your biscuit? Pigs in your blanket?"

Katie stared. First of all, was he serious? And second of all, she was used to doctors talking to her mom, as if they spoke a different language than Katie and needed an interpreter. And sometimes, they did. Katie wasn't sure what to do with a doctor who asked her questions. Especially questions like that.

"She had a transplant seven years ago," said Katie's mom, gripping her note-taking pencil so tightly Katie was afraid she might snap it in half. "And she has a faulty mitral valve."

"Well, of course," the doctor said, and he snuck Katie a smile. "I've read all about that in her chart."

It was hard not to feel a little better when your new doctor was wearing alligator scrubs and didn't seem the slightest bit worried.

Dr. Samha listened to Katie's heart, of course, and took her temperature. He weighed her and measured her height. "You're pocket-size!" he declared. "Perfect for a ten-year-old." He checked the chart. "But you're growing, and that's good. Still staying away from contact sports?" he asked. "No tackle football or tackle tennis?"

Katie shook her head.

"We're very careful," said her mom. "Extra careful. We know how vulnerable she is."

"That's good," said Dr. Samha, looking serious for the first time.

Not always, thought Katie. She cleared her throat.

"What about ice-skating?" she asked.

"No ice-skating," said Katie's mom, before Dr. Samha could even answer. "Absolutely not."

Dr. Samha looked back and forth between the two of them. "I believe I will let you and your mother sort that out. But it might be best to be careful until we see what these tests say. Okay?"

Which meant no skating. They never got all the results

back until at least a couple of weeks had passed, so Katie had lost again.

Dr. Samha tapped the screen of his tablet. "I'm not sure her chart transferred properly," he said, showing them a big, blank rectangle in the middle. "There's nothing here for family medical history. And I know this girl has a family." He gave Katie a wink, and she looked down at her lap.

"Of course she has a family." Katie's mom started to pop out of her chair, but Katie's dad put his hand on her arm.

"Katie is adopted," he said. "We don't know anything about her birth family."

Dr. Samha fiddled with his tablet and bowed his head. "Of course. So sorry. So sorry."

"It's all right," said her dad.

But it wasn't. Katie had come to the doctor hoping for good news, and he'd told her to keep holding back. He'd shown her a whole part of her past she'd never realized she should be worried about.

What if her birth family had scary diseases and the heart was only the beginning? Katie would never know until it was too late. Her mom's words sliced through her again.

It all depends.

It all depended, all right. On things Katie couldn't control, like her heart, and things she couldn't know, like her past.

That night, Katie and her parents curled up together in front of the TV. At every commercial break, there was Elena Korsikova and her stupid quadruple toe loop.

Except it wasn't stupid. It was magnificent. She leaped from the ice in her red firebird costume, turning and turning and turning and turning. Katie loved how it was the moment she landed and spread her wings that you got the feeling she had really taken flight. That was the moment they'd captured in the poster.

Babushka's words echoed in her mind.

If you find the feather of a firebird, a great quest has found you. You must return the feather to find your destiny, to make all your dreams come true. It is never easy, and it almost never works. It is a lonely and dangerous task. But you must try.

Even if she didn't believe in the magic part, Katie felt the truth in the story. In the corner of her homework, she drew a bird like the one on her pocket watch. It couldn't be a firebird, could it?

From the moment she'd found the box, Katie had felt

something awaken inside her. But the bigger words—quest, destiny, dreams coming true—seemed so far beyond what she could hope for. Somehow, she'd gotten stuck in the lonely and dangerous part.

When he saw her drawing, Katie's dad told her about the phoenix—another fiery bird reborn from its own ashes, able to give light and life. Katie's worry eased a little as she felt the truth in that story too. Sometimes your life could start again.

Later, when Katie's dad came in to tell her good night, he held the two Thankfuls they'd read at dinner. "What are the odds," he asked, "that we would both read the 'new heart' Thankful on the same night? And that it would happen right after we met your new cardiologist?"

Katie didn't answer. It did seem like a coincidence, but not necessarily a happy one.

"Well, then," he said, as he bent his achy knees and sat at the edge of her bed. "Perhaps you don't want to talk about the doctor, do you?"

Katie shook her head.

He cleared his throat. "Or the fact that you'd probably better not go on that field trip. I'm so sorry."

"That's what I figured," Katie said. "Maybe next time."

Her dad laid the Thankful links on her nightstand and lined them up neatly. "Definitely next time." He didn't pretend like that was good enough, and Katie was glad for that. "Let's change the subject. Did you know I've forgotten to ask what you want for Christmas? What kind of a father am I?"

"The best kind," Katie said, and she meant it. "But I'm not sure you want to know what I want for Christmas."

Her dad smiled. "Try me."

Katie looked away. "Ice skates. That's all I want."

"Oh, my girl," he said. "I would give them to you in a heartbeat if I could."

A heartbeat. It was just a saying, since heartbeats were supposed to be so quick and insignificant. Still, she wished he'd picked another word.

"Are you sure that's all you want?" he asked. "I thought I had an even better idea, but if that's all you want . . ."

Katie's mind raced. Had she forgotten something better she'd already hinted at? "Well, I wouldn't turn down another gift, I guess."

Her dad laughed. "That's my girl. Now, I don't want you to worry one bit about all this medical stuff. Take care of yourself—that's your job. The worrying is your mother's job, and mine. And another thing: don't worry about that history nonsense."

Katie had never thought she'd hear her history professor dad say those words. She pictured the blank spot on Dr. Samha's tablet, white as snow and glowing with all the space where her birth family should have been.

Her dad took both her hands and laced his fingers through hers. "We're connected, you know. You have a family history, because you're part of this family." He held up one pair of hands. "My pioneer ancestors are yours too. They were tough, just like you. They lived in caves their first winter out west, and when spring came, they realized they'd been sharing the caves with a hundred hibernating rattlesnakes. So they ate a few for supper and chased the rest away."

Katie shivered. She wasn't sure she was that tough.

"And your mother's family," he said, holding up her other hand in his. "Oh, you are smart like them. Did you know her great-grandfather, your great-*great*-grandfather, was a famous scientist? He invented a way to purify water that still saves lives today!"

After Katie's dad had left, she tried to imagine those words in the blank space on Dr. Samha's screen. *Family history: Tough as a pioneer. Smart as a scientist.* She imagined telling those stories to her own children, or somebody telling her grandchildren those things about her someday.

But as much as she wanted to, Katie couldn't hold on to those stories and claim them as her own. She couldn't quite believe those things about her heart or her mind.

Who was she, then?

Katie still hadn't found any kind of answer when her mom came in much later and sat in the rocking chair beside her bed.

"Sweetheart," she whispered. "Are you still awake?"

"Yes."

In the darkness, Katie heard the rhythm of the *brim-brum* as the chair began to rock. "Go to sleep, my love. The morning is wiser than the evening."

Deep under the covers, Katie pulled her watch closer. She knew her mom would always be there, willing to carry both their worries. So after a while, Katie gave them over and closed her eyes.

And in her dreams, she skated.

Ana

Chapter 12

THE MORNING OF the big fifth-grade skating trip, Ana tried to hustle Mikey along so maybe they'd get to school early for once. It didn't work.

Mikey added the new candle they'd light that night at the very end of the menorah.

"No," she sighed. "You have to put it in the next empty spot." Babushka would disapprove if they left the menorah like that. In fact, Ana was starting to lose track of all the things Babushka disapproved of. The list was too long and only getting longer.

She disapproved of their totally unkosher kitchen.

She disapproved of Hanukkah presents.

And she definitely disapproved of their relaxing Saturdays.

"Instead of buying them things they don't need," she'd said, "take these children to the synagogue and give them the gifts of God."

So the first Saturday of December, when Ana should have been hanging out at Katie's house, they'd all dressed up and gone to services. The most annoying part of all was how much Ana actually liked it. She loved the way everybody seemed to know what to do, and it wasn't too hard for her to figure out when to pray and what to say either, even though she was new. Plus, the old ladies were so nice, and when they told her what a good girl she was, Ana sort of believed them. She was almost looking forward to going tomorrow.

But not as much as she was looking forward to the field trip today, if she could ever get Mikey out of the house.

Mikey wiggled one of the Hanukkah candles. "Are you sure I can't wish on these too? I think I'd wish to be a superhero."

Ana held out his coat. "They're not birthday candles. And the puck wasn't supposed to be for wishes either. You're just supposed to tell it when you have a problem."

Mikey pointed to a hole in his jeans. "This is a problem. Superheroes don't have holes in their pants."

Ana rolled her eyes. "Superheroes don't even wear pants!"

Mikey looked a little disturbed by that, so Ana decided to change the subject. "Plus, if you're going to be a superhero, you'll need a superpower first."

"Like the puck?" he asked.

"No, Mikey. A superpower is something you can *do*, not something you *have*."

Mikey nodded, letting it soak in. He began putting on his boots in little-kid slow motion.

"Babushka says if I want new pants, I have to get a job so I can pay for them myself. And Jarek says kids with holes in their pants pee their pants too."

Sometimes Ana wanted to give Jarek a kick in the pants. What kind of fifth grader picked on a first grader?

"You know how I got that hole?" Mikey asked. "Jarek tripped me on the playground. He said nobody in my family can stay up on the ice."

Ana grabbed Mikey's other boot and started shoving his foot inside. "Don't talk to him. And definitely don't tell him about the Winter Classic or the puck or any of that stuff or he'll ruin that too."

Mikey paused with his bootlaces half-tied. "Are you sure it still counts as the wish coming true if your sister makes it happen?" he asked.

"It totally counts." If only Mikey knew how much every wish depended on her.

"Why don't you ever wish on the puck?"

Ana shrugged. "Because I don't need anything."

That wasn't true. She needed to remember the rules for multiplying and dividing fractions. She needed to fill in the holes of her put-the-family-back-together plan.

But right now, she just needed to not miss the field trip. Ana grabbed her skate bag and headed for the front door, but Babushka was there, blocking the way.

Of course she was.

"I find this in your backpack," she said, shaking a blue paper Ana had hoped she'd never find. "Parents need to help with field trip. Your parents cannot come, so I come."

"Um, no." Ana grabbed the paper from Babushka. "I think they have plenty of volunteers now. This is old."

Babushka's mouth drew into a thin line. "Paper is from yesterday. I check your backpack every day."

"It's *my* backpack!" she said. "You can't just open it up. It's private property."

"Hmm." Babushka stroked her chin with long, bony fingers. "Like my suitcase?"

"That's different," Ana spluttered. She shouldn't even be having this fight, but she couldn't back down either.

Then there was her mom, sneaking Ana a tired smile. "Babushka," she said, in a voice like honey, "how are you?"

Babushka thought a moment. "Normal."

If you say so, thought Ana.

Her mom took Babushka by the elbow. "I wanted to ask you about the latkes for tonight. I thought we could get them at Mary's in the village."

"Ack!" said Babushka as she walked away. "Latkes from a shiksa's bakery?" She shook a finger at Ana and Mikey. "You are lucky I am here to save you from this, while all you do is make trouble."

As Babushka smacked her lips at her own sour words,

Ana's mom turned back with another smile, a little brighter this time. "We'll see you after school," she said. "Have fun."

Ana had never wanted to hug her mom so hard. Every once in a while she showed flashes of her real self—the one who understood her kids and actually took care of them. That little move was almost enough to make Ana forgive her for all the times she hadn't saved them from Babushka, for all the times lately she hadn't really been there at all.

The frost that had formed between Ana and Katie seemed to be thawing again as they boarded the bus for the field trip.

"I can't believe your mom said yes."

Katie looked away. "She didn't. Not exactly."

"Oooh, I gotcha. Don't worry. My lips are zipped."

Apparently Katie's lips were zipped too. She was silent the whole bus ride over, and when they got to the rink, she just sat there, staring at her skates. Technically, they were Ana's old skates from two winters ago, but Katie had small feet. She kind of had small everything.

Ana could already hear kids shouting and laughing out on the ice. Were they picking teams for pick-up hockey?

Hopefully Sadie, the next-best fifth grader, would ask Ana to play. Except now that Ana didn't play, Sadie was the best.

So maybe Sadie wouldn't ask.

Ana had to get out there.

"You put your feet inside," she said to Katie. "And you lace them up."

When Katie looked up, her face was white as the ice. "I know," she said. "I'm getting ready."

"Getting what ready?" Ana asked.

"My . . . self." Katie started loosening the laces of one of the skates, slow as could be. It felt like watching Mikey put his boots on all over again. But now that Ana thought about it, Katie did lots of things slowly. Had she ever even seen Katie run?

Katie hesitated. "I thought maybe your grandma would come."

"She wanted to, but my mom distracted her. Thank goodness."

"Oh." Katie's gaze dropped. "I thought maybe I could talk to her. So she wouldn't be lonely, or something."

Ana laughed. "Good one. She likes to be alone, and I know you've been dying to skate."

More kids poured past them and headed for the ice. Ana glanced over and saw all the other fifth graders in their brightly colored coats, swirling around like a whirlpool. There went Jarek and Marcus, playing a two-person version of crack the whip that didn't look totally safe for anybody. They bumped into a kid who was limping along the edge and barely tossed a "sorry" over their shoulders as they skated away.

Then there went Sadie, faster than last year, moving as easily as water down a stream. Maybe she'd be the best fifth-grade hockey player now even if Ana hadn't quit.

Ana turned away. She'd had to give up the thing she loved, just because her dad had given up on them. But now that he would be coming back, Ana ached more than ever to play again. She glanced back at Katie, who was barely tying up her first skate.

"Do you want me to wait?"

Katie waved her away. "No, go out there. I want to watch and learn for a minute."

Ana stepped onto the ice, and all the friction that had held her back vanished. She spotted the poor kid who'd gotten bumped into, still frozen with his back to the boards. She slapped him on the shoulder as she skated past. "Right back out there and try again," she said, and once the words were out, they sounded familiar. Was that what her dad had said when he'd taught her? Or had it been her mom?

There wasn't time to wonder. Off she went, once, twice, three times around the rink. Ana shivered with the same-but-different feeling of it all—the thrill and speed she'd loved when she played, but now without all the pads and pressure and coaches and rules.

Ana felt totally free until she realized Katie still wasn't anywhere on the ice, which she probably should have noticed before. As she glided back over to the benches, her old skates peeked out at her from behind a trash can. So where was Katie?

In spite of what Ana had said, Katie was the brave one a lot of the time. She was the one who was willing to ask the teacher when something didn't make sense or stick up for somebody who was getting picked on.

Ana scanned the empty locker room, then poked her head into the bathroom. "Katie?"

Katie's voice came, thin and scared, from the last stall. "I'm almost done."

Ana felt awkward asking, but she felt even more

impatient. "Everything okay in there?"

"Yes."

"So what are you doing? Writing a novel? Counting to a billion?" She felt her face flush as another thought came to her. "Is it a problem with your . . . plumbing?"

The door opened and Katie's face appeared, bright red too. "Just . . . never mind. I wasn't even going to the bathroom."

If she wasn't going to the bathroom, why spend ten minutes in the stinky stall?

Then Ana knew. Katie was scared. And even though Ana was a good friend, she'd been dealing with other people's problems way too much lately. All she wanted was to think about herself and have fun for one stinking day.

"If you don't dare skate, why have you been yakking about it for the last two weeks?" The words felt like a slap when they came out of her mouth, but Ana wasn't entirely sorry she'd said them.

"I'm going to skate," Katie said, but Ana could tell neither one of them believed it.

"If you say so."

Katie stepped to the sink and scrubbed her hands. "Just give me a second." She didn't look up. She was blinking a lot, and she just kept scrubbing.

Oh, flip. Ana should have recognized Mikey's classic trying-not-to-cry signs earlier. She wanted to backpedal, but she couldn't think of a thing to say that would make it better.

"Okay, well, I'll be out there. Whenever you're ready."

As she waited, Ana tried to put herself in Katie's shoes. Skates. Whatever. She remembered the first time she'd gone out onto the ice—how her parents had each held one of her hands the whole afternoon. Maybe it was easier to be brave when it wasn't so easy to fall.

Katie appeared at the edge of the rink. She looked straight ahead and hooked her gloved fingers around Ana's, then took her first wobbly steps onto the ice. Right, left. Right, left. More like limping than gliding, but that was the way to start.

"I'm skating," Katie whispered. The worry melted from her face and she looked at Ana, almost like she needed to make sure it was true.

"You're skating," Ana said. "You're doing fine." Gradually, the steps turned to slides and the blood began to return to Ana's fingers as Katie's grip loosened. After a few laps, she barely used Ana for balance at all, and the current of kids didn't have to part around them so much anymore.

"Want to let go?"

"Almost," Katie said.

"Take your time," Ana said. "Or . . ."

She pulled Katie along until they had enough momentum, then reached for her other hand. "Hold on," she said. "And trust me."

Together, Ana and Katie spun toward the center of the rink, around and around like figures in a music box with their hair flying straight out behind them. Katie broke into the biggest grin Ana had seen all day.

"That's what I came here for," Katie said. "That feeling right there." A tiny line of worry appeared on her forehead. "But my pulse is kind of high."

Ana spun around and skated backward in front of Katie. "Good! It's supposed to be! You don't get a certain number of heartbeats, you know." Ana felt her own heart thumping inside her, telling her she was right. "You can't save them up. When it's beating hard like that, it's getting stronger. It's putting heartbeats in the bank."

Katie seemed to think about that. "Maybe you're right," she admitted.

So they got themselves undizzy and did it again. After

that, Katie was ready to skate on her own. She never went fast, and Ana lapped her more than once, but it sure seemed to be fast enough.

Ana heard a familiar laugh behind her. Sadie. She felt a tug on her hood and the chill of something wet against her back. She whipped around to find Sadie with a sneaky smile on her face and ice shavings stuck to her gloves.

It had been their joke, and Ana had totally forgotten about it. Two seasons ago, when they'd been on the same team, they'd wait for the goalie to rough up the ice in front of the goal, then sneak the shavings into each other's jerseys.

Ana shivered. "You're so dead."

"Ha! No way. You'll never get me now that I suspect it."

The girls fell into stride next to each other. "No hockey today?" Ana asked.

"Nah," said Sadie. "Too many kids and not enough space."

Regret plucked inside Ana. Now that she couldn't play today, she wanted to more than ever.

"We miss you," Sadie said. "Are you playing next season?"

"Yes," said Ana. There was no question about it now.

"So if you want to be MVP, you'd better make it happen this year."

Sadie laughed. She slide-stopped in front of Ana, then stooped to pick up the shavings. "We've got to team up and get somebody else now. Want to?" She pointed at Katie and wiggled her eyebrows.

Even though Sadie was just having fun, Ana got a shiver that seemed to say it was a terrible idea. She almost tried to stop her. But she didn't, and Sadie was halfway around the rink by the time she caught up with Katie. Ana watched as Sadie reached up with her empty hand and pulled out Katie's hood, then dumped the ice shavings down her coat.

Katie cried out like a wounded animal. She tripped and groped toward the wall, then fell against it. Ana tried to skate toward her, but before she could reach her, Katie spun around and started skating back toward the benches, clutching her chest and moving straight against the stream of people.

"Katie!" Ana shouted. "Go the other way! You're going to get hurt!"

Jarek and Marcus turned their heads to see what Ana was yelling about, but they didn't slow down. So really, it was Ana's fault. And their fault. And Sadie's fault.

It was all of their fault that the boys crashed into Katie and knocked her, headfirst, down to the ice. Ana screamed and raced over, and by the time she got there, Katie was lying limp with her eyes closed and a circle of blood blooming from underneath her hat.

Katie

Chapter 13

VOICES SWIRLED.

The whole world was cold and hard and shifting.

When Katie opened her eyes, five dark shapes hovered over her. One by one, they came into focus: Ana, then Sadie from the class next door, then Jarek and Marcus, and finally a man with an official-looking name tag.

Katie's head throbbed and her back hurt and her feet

seemed weirdly heavy. She closed her eyes again and listened to her heart.

Normal. It was back to normal. She wasn't sure what had happened out on the ice, but it had been scary.

Sadie grabbed her hand. "Katie, I'm so sorry! I'll never do that again! Please don't die!"

"Holy flip, you're worse than Mikey," Ana said. "She's not going to die."

Katie wished she could have a recording of those words, in that voice, to play every time she went to a doctor or a hospital. Ana seemed so sure.

"I'm not going to die," Katie finally agreed. "Not until my mom finds out, anyway."

Ana laughed, and so did everybody else. The man with the name tag leaned over her. "Give yourself a second, and then I'm going to sit you up. You might need a butterfly bandage on your head." He turned to the kids circled around. "I knew you guys needed more chaperones. No more ice down people's coats."

It was just ice, Katie thought.

As she'd skated, Katie had felt like a different person, almost like she was soaring above the ice instead of across it. But when she'd felt the shock of cold down her back, she'd come crashing down, knowing her mom was right and her heart couldn't handle it.

Except, she realized, her heart *could* handle it. The skating, the shock, even hitting her head—all that, and her heart still beat a steady rhythm inside her. Now that she thought about it, her heart hadn't been the problem at all. Only her fear.

Katie tried to smile as she sat up, but the swirl of the skaters around them and the slippery ice made everything spin.

"Take your time," the man said, as one of the chaperones hovered in the background. "You lost quite a bit of blood."

"I'm okay," she said. "Ana will take care of me."

"You'll need to call your mom," the man said. "Even if she'll be mad. Want to use my phone?"

"Not yet," Katie said quickly. "Let me clean up first. I can borrow Ms. Decker's phone."

It was a careful half-truth. She *could* borrow Ms. Decker's phone, but that didn't mean she would. And it wasn't the first half-truth she'd told that day.

Katie had handed the permission slip to her mom just this morning. "I guess you have to get it signed even if you're staying," she'd said. It was true, even if Katie didn't plan on being one of the kids left behind. Then, with her bedroom door locked tight, she'd erased the mark and checked the other box. It had all gone so smoothly, right up until the crash.

Katie grabbed the man's arm to steady herself as she stood, and he helped her hobble to the first-aid station. He cleaned the wound with a special wipe and stuck a butterfly bandage across it, then helped her to the locker room before heading back over to supervise everybody else.

Ana trashed the paper towels she'd been holding against Katie's head.

"I have to admit, that was pretty impressive. We already threw your hat away. Hope that's okay." She helped Katie sit down and started unlacing her skates. "And don't worry, I won't tell your mom." Her mouth turned up into a crooked, sneaky smile. "I finally feel like you've got a good secret for me to keep."

Katie tried to ignore the guilt that twisted inside her. She wanted to tell Ana everything, but the timing still seemed all wrong.

"How bad is it?" she asked.

Ana held up a skate and showed Katie her reflection in

the shiny blade. Even in such a thin strip, the gash looked red and raw and definitely not small.

"Oh, shoot. Look at me. This is bad."

Ana took the skate away and shrugged. "I've had worse," she said. "It won't even scar, I bet. If you had bangs, it'd be fine." Ana's eyes brightened. "Hey, want me to cut you some bangs?"

Katie shook her head. "Can I have your hat?"

Ana took off her beanie and tossed it over. "My gift to you. Now you owe me one."

"I have a gift, actually," Katie said. "I wasn't sure when to give it to you since I've never had a friend who celebrated Hanukkah before."

"Now," Ana said. "The perfect time is now. Geez, I was just kidding about owing me, but go for it."

Katie stretched the beanie carefully around her head and over her wound. Even in the locker room, the gentle pressure and the fact that the gash was hidden made her feel much safer. She found the locker they'd stashed their stuff in and grabbed the silver-wrapped box from her bag.

Ana tore off the wrapping and lifted the lid. "Wow! I mean, wow! They're so pretty." She took the bracelets from their box. "Pretty's not usually my thing, but these are awesome." The bracelets flashed and sparkled, even in the light of the locker room, as Ana slipped one onto each wrist and twisted them around.

Katie felt a wash of relief. Ana loved them. Maybe everything could be back to normal now. She reached for the bracelets. "Can I show you something?"

Ana slid off the bracelets and laid them in Katie's palm. Katie lined up the two small circles until they looked like one. "If you turn them just right, they connect to each other and . . ." She aligned each red heart with its matching jewel on the other bracelet until they snapped perfectly inside one another.

"Oh, wow!" Ana leaned way over. "That's awesome."

Getting the bracelets to fit together had been the hardest part, and Katie had needed to change each one in little, imperceptible ways. She'd used the whole bag of special snap-together beads her dad had brought her from England. She'd worked so hard on those bracelets that suddenly she wasn't even sure she wanted to give them away.

Ana took the bracelets and popped them apart, heart by heart. She handed one to Katie. "They'll be like best friend bracelets. We can wear them all the time so it's official."

Katie hadn't even thought of that before, and it was such a nice idea. The bracelets seemed to have finally fixed all that had been unsettled between them for the last two weeks, like the last beads snapping into place. But something at the back of Katie's brain tried to tell her the bracelets belonged together, and she wished she'd kept them both.

Stop. Katie thought the word so strongly she almost said it out loud. It had to be that she just wasn't feeling right.

"Best friends for sure. Thanks, Ana. Um, is it almost time to go?" she asked. "I'm not feeling so good."

Ana gave Katie a soft squeeze on the shoulder. "I'll go ask a teacher. Take it easy, best friend."

Katie leaned her head back against the lockers, wondering what was wrong with her lately. Why couldn't she feel like anything was enough? A healthy new heart and almost-perfect grades; one bracelet or one best friend or one mom who loved her? Why did it feel like so much was still missing?

Katie closed her eyes most of the bus ride back and dreamed of crawling into her bed. But when she came through the door after school, her mom was waiting in the kitchen.

"How was your day?"

"Great," Katie said, and the wound hidden under her hat gave a little throb. Her mom could never know about today. Never. Katie gave a gentle nod at the paper in her mom's hand. "What's that?"

"A surprise for you. A good one."

Katie unfolded the paper with shaky fingers.

BOSTON BALLET STAGES STUNNING PRODUCTION OF *THE NUTCRACKER*

Katie's thoughts flew to the nutcracker from the attic. She could still picture its soldier's uniform and its wobbly jaw with perfectly painted teeth, and suddenly she longed to see it and hold it again.

Katie's mom reached over and squeezed her hand. "I know how hard it must have been to miss that field trip, so I called and got us tickets! Just in time, too—they only had a few left for tonight."

Guilt scratched inside Katie. Her secret wanted to come out so badly. But how could she let her mom down? And how could she risk being held even more tightly after the freedom she'd felt on the ice today?

"Wow, Mom. Thanks." Any other words might lead to the terrible truth.

"We'll get pizza and ice cream first at Picco's. It will be our special date, and maybe it can even become our new Christmas tradition. Your dad doesn't mind sitting this one out." She leaned forward with the smallest frown on her face. "What happened to your hat?"

Katie's fingers flew to her forehead, expecting to feel a warm, wet circle of blood. Just as her heart began to gallop, she realized what her mom meant.

"Oh, this is Ana's hat. We decided to trade. For fun."

"Hmm," said her mom. "Well, be sure you trade back. Now go get ready! We'll need to leave early to get a parking spot, and I can't wait for a date with my girl."

With the bathroom door locked behind her, Katie carefully pulled off Ana's hat. The wound growled back at her from the mirror, scary and brown and gross. She folded up a tissue and darted it under the stream from the faucet, then dabbed at her forehead. Once all the dried blood and thin hairs of hat fuzz were off, it didn't seem nearly as bad. Her mom might not even notice it, if Katie took off the tiny butterfly bandage.

So she pinched the corner of the bandage and peeled it from her skin. *Much, much better.* The gash could almost pass for a scratch now, and she could think of a good explanation for a scratch, maybe even one that wouldn't be a total lie.

In her bedroom, Katie slipped into the skirt her mom had laid out for her, then pulled a sweater over her head. But as she did it, she felt something else pull too, and something wet and warm trickled down her temple.

With the beanie pressed to her head again, Katie rushed to the bathroom and looked in the mirror. Big drops of blood oozed from the end of the gash. She grabbed a washcloth and held it to her forehead, then checked her sweater. *Clean.* She pressed the washcloth against the gash for fifty heartbeats before pulling it away.

The bleeding had stopped. She was okay.

"Sweetheart?" Her mom knocked softly on the door. "Are you almost ready?"

"Just a second!" Katie tried to stick the butterfly bandage back on, but it wasn't quite as sticky as before. She rummaged around in the drawer until she found regular Band-Aids and taped one across the wound.

Katie begged her heart to stay steady and her head to stop bleeding as she rushed back to her room and scanned her closet, desperate for anything that might cover the bandage. Finally, Katie discovered the thin scarf she'd braided from colorful strips of her family's old T-shirts. If she stretched it just right, she could wrap it around herself like a headband.

Okay, a long, awkward headband that, when she checked the mirror, did not look anything close to normal and definitely didn't match her clothes.

Oh well. It would have to work.

Katie's parents raised their eyebrows a little when they saw her new look.

"Well, if I'd known we could go in costume," her dad said with a wink, "I might have joined you."

Katie's mom planted her fists on her hips. "I think the scarf is lovely, and you're not invited. You always make fun of the story."

Katie's dad switched to his storytelling voice. "Once there was a girl named Clara who wore her nightgown twenty-four/seven."

"Dad!" Katie protested.

"Once there was a toymaker who made creepy, life-size clown dolls, and people actually invited him to their fancy parties."

"Yes," Katie's mom said, swatting him with her dish towel. "We all know your version, and that's why you're not invited."

"It's giant dancing dolls and mice!" Katie's dad threw his hands up. "It's grown men running around in matching shirts and tight pants! Which is fine, but not for me."

"Yes, I can see that." Katie's mom rolled her eyes at the football game he was watching, where dozens of grown men ran around in matching shirts and tight pants. "Katie, are you ready to go?"

Katie could see her mom's lips itching to say something more about her scarf, but she bit back the words.

"I'm ready," Katie said, even though she knew she'd spend half the evening hoping she wasn't bleeding through the scarf.

Except she didn't. Once they were at the restaurant, she only thought about thin-crust pizza and buttery breadsticks and peppermint snowflake ice cream. And once they were at the ballet, she only thought about the ballet.

How incredible the costumes were—each one with its own universe of beads and fabrics and bright embroidery. How the scenery transformed the stage from a fancy party to an enchanted forest to a palace of ice, and Katie took every step of the journey. And the theater itself—ivory and gold and the very richest reds. A ceiling that seemed as vast and grand as the sky.

The story, too, was beautiful, no matter what her dad said. Katie had never known you could tell such a story without a single word, but the movement and music were more than enough. And sometimes when the dancers glided across the stage, it looked almost like skating.

That part made Katie think about her fall, just a little, but mostly it made her remember the moment when Ana had taken her hands and spun her around and she had finally, finally felt like she could move freely.

In spite of it all, she'd done it today. She'd skated. And maybe someday, if she could get herself fixed up and a little stronger, she could dance too.

Katie slipped off her bracelet and smoothed her thumb across the beads. She laid her head on her mom's shoulder. Maybe she didn't have to be the snow child forever, or the lonely firebird. Maybe she could be this girl, this Clara, strong and graceful and confident.

As the broken toy was mended and came to life onstage, as the little girl became a princess, as the music rose and swirled around Katie and inside her, anything seemed possible.

Ana

Chapter 14

FOR THE REST of the day, Ana worried about Katie. Every time she'd almost forget, the bracelet would remind her, its red beads like drops of blood around her wrist. Even though Katie had seemed fine on the bus ride back, the image of her lying on the ice kept popping up in Ana's brain. There had been so much blood—more than Ana had ever seen in any of her hockey games—and she couldn't help remembering how she'd talked Katie into being out on the ice in the first place.

By the time she'd gagged down Babushka's dinner—something like Jell-O, but with meat in it. Meat!—Ana couldn't take it anymore. She needed to check in with Katie, just to be sure. This was officially an emergency. As soon as she'd finished the dishes, Ana put two candles in her window. She'd go down to the pond as soon as she saw Katie come out the door.

Any second now.

Any second now.

Aaaaany second now.

Ana started to panic. Katie was always in her room by eight o'clock. What if she'd passed out again and her parents weren't paying attention? Ana had better check on her.

"Where are you going?" Mikey asked as Ana pulled on her snow boots.

"Over to Katie's," she said. "Shhh." If Babushka thought Ana had a free second, she'd put her straight back to work.

Mikey started to pull the coat closet open, but Ana pushed it shut. "I'd better go by myself this time, buddy. She might be hurt."

"She might be hurt?" Mikey's voice was pinched and scared. "Is she going to have to go to the hospital?"

"Shhh, Mikey. She's fine." Mikey had been crazy-afraid of hospitals ever since they'd visited their dad there after a bad concussion and he hadn't remembered them. (It probably hadn't helped that he'd been missing four teeth too.) If there was something wrong with Katie, Mikey was the last person who should be there.

"I'll be back soon, buddy, but I need you to cover for me. You've got to stay here with Babushka."

Mikey's jaw dropped. "What?"

"If you show her what a good little boy you are, she'll see that we're fine and she'll go home soon. Listen to her stories. Or sing her a song! Maybe that one from synagogue about the little candle."

Mikey wrinkled his nose. "I'm not singing."

"Okay, well, there are other ways. You could also rub her feet or paint her toenails."

Mikey shook his head.

"Shave her armpits? Wash her underwear?"

"Ana!" Mikey covered his ears. "You can't make me do any of that!" He ran upstairs to his room, which meant he didn't whine or beg or even notice when Ana left for

Katie's house without him.

It was only snowing a little, tiny flakes that melted as soon as they touched Ana's skin or even her coat. She made it to Katie's house in record time and knocked as loudly as she could. It felt weird not to walk right in, but she'd never come over this late before. She waited patiently on the porch while slow footsteps creaked toward the front door.

Katie's dad.

"Ana," he said as she zipped past him and into the house. "Come in, won't you?"

Since she was already in, she glanced back to make sure he was kidding. She was a little surprised he knew her name. She tried to remember whether her dad had ever known any of her friends' first names. It seemed like he'd barely known the last names on their jerseys. But they could fix that too, when he came back.

"Katie's not here right now," Mr. Burton said. "She went downtown with her mother."

"Downtown again? To the hospital?" Ana asked, afraid of the answer.

"Oh, no," said Mr. Burton. "Nothing like that. They're at the ballet."

Ana realized she'd made a face when Mr. Burton

answered, "My feelings exactly. Even if I could stay awake that late."

"Is it the one with the creepy doll?" Ana asked.

"Yes," he answered. "But there are a few of those. It's the one where the girl's best friend is a nutcracker, and the poor thing's head snaps off."

Ana's heart pounded. Did he mean the *girl's* head snapped off? Did Katie's dad know about her accident? Ana wouldn't give anything away, just in case.

"Yeah, that's pretty hilarious." She stopped. "I mean, that's not funny at all. Head injuries are serious. At least, that's what I've heard." *Oh my gosh, Ana. Stop talking right now.* Beads of sweat began to form at the back of her neck.

But Katie's dad didn't seem to notice. "I can tell her you stopped by, or you're welcome to leave a note. There's a pad and pencil by the bulletin board."

"I'll leave her a note," Ana said. "Thanks." She turned to the TV. "Bowl games already?"

"Just like Christmas decorations in stores, huh? Earlier every year, and more of them."

He seemed pretty happy about that as he began rinsing dishes, humming something Christmassy and sort of familiar.

Ana soaked in the rich, homey smell of whatever Mr. Burton had just eaten for dinner. She shrugged off her coat and hung it over the back of a chair, then grabbed the paper and pencil.

While she was at it, Ana couldn't help but notice the big bulletin board on the kitchen wall. It was filled with photographs of Katie, drawings by Katie, and every one of Katie's hundred-percent tests and perfect report cards. The ballet tickets would probably end up there, a happy reminder of the special night between Katie and her mom.

Meanwhile, Ana's mom didn't even talk to her half the time. How long since the two of them had done something like that? Had they ever?

All the worry Ana had been spending on her best friend slowly turned to a sad kind of wishing. Not jealous, really—not wishing she could take what Katie had. Only wishing somehow she could have it too.

You will, she told herself. *Starting on New Year's.* But she still wasn't quite back to believing it.

Ana settled down at the kitchen table to write the note. *Dear Katie,* she began. *Your parents love you more than anything. That's so lucky.* Then she remembered why she'd come over in the first place. *I'm sorry you got hurt, but I*

172

know you'll get better soon. I hope you still trust me, because I trust you. And I take back what I said before about you needing to find some courage. Just stay safe, okay? You're already brave.
Ana

From the other room, Ana could hear a mix of stats and jokes that meant a halftime report. Even though they were talking about football and not hockey (which didn't even have halftime, just intermissions), her ears still perked up every time she heard words like "goal" or "penalty."

Outside the kitchen window, the snow had begun to fall in thick, heavy flakes. Ana looked back at the notepad. She'd done what she came here to do, and Katie was fine. She should get her coat and go home.

But then Mr. Burton set a round golden roll and a cup of creamy potato soup next to her.

"Made the soup myself," he said, before returning to his humming and his dishes.

It would be rude to just get up and leave. So Ana ate, trying not to be jealous of Katie. It was getting harder, though. The tiny, twinkling lights all around. The soft music and the sweet smells of Mrs. Burton's baking, still lingering even when she wasn't home. A dad who made thick, amazing soup for his daughter instead of leaving her behind to chase more minutes on the ice. *This* was what a home was supposed to feel like.

Her home had been like that, sort of, only last year. They'd lit the menorah together and eaten latkes (from a shiksa's bakery) and filled four chairs with the right four bodies. But this year, Babushka's latkes had been heavy and hard, and it still gave Ana a little shock sometimes to see her sitting in her dad's old chair.

Ana reread her note to Katie, then folded it in half. "I'll go put this upstairs," she said to Mr. Burton. He was done with the dishes now, and he smiled and nodded at her as he wiped his hands on a towel.

"I'm headed up to the attic myself, next commercial break," he said. "You won't mind letting yourself out if I'm still up there? I take it you know the way?"

Ana nodded. "Not a problem. And thanks."

Upstairs in Katie's bedroom, Ana felt a little spark of surprise to see her own hat laid on the dresser, like a part of her had already found its place here. If somebody bled on your hat, did that make you blood sisters? Probably.

Even though blood sisters went a step or two past best friends, Ana was glad she didn't see Katie's half of the bracelet lying around. Hopefully Katie had worn it to the ballet. Hopefully she would always wear it, and her family wouldn't pick up and move again, leaving Ana behind.

Mr. Burton passed by the doorway with a roll of wrapping paper in one hand and tape and scissors in the other, just carrying on with his business as though Ana belonged in this house.

And suddenly, fiercely, she wished she did.

After Mr. Burton disappeared up the attic stairs, Ana turned off Katie's lights. The colored bulbs around Katie's window made the perfect frame for the paper snowflakes they'd cut out together at Thanksgiving and the great white flakes drifting down outside. And it was so quiet and peaceful with no Mikey around.

Ana tiptoed over to Katie's bed and only hesitated a second before lying carefully on top of the quilt. *This is what it feels like,* she thought. *To live the perfect life as the perfect daughter in this perfect family.*

Something, though, didn't feel quite so perfect. A lump, smaller than the hockey puck, dug into Ana's ribs. She rolled over and reached under the covers, soft and warm even without anybody inside.

A shock of recognition raced through Ana as she stared down at the pocket watch. What the heck was it doing here?

Ana paused. Had Babushka given it to Katie? She must have. But why? When?

Ana squeezed her eyes shut. She'd been ready to get rid of Babushka since the moment she'd arrived, and she'd never been a watch person at all. So why did it hurt so much to find this watch here?

Because Katie already had everything. And on top of that, she was so good that even Babushka loved her and wanted to give her things. So good, even Ana's mom wanted to talk to her and hug her.

If Ana had been that good, would her family have stayed together?

Ana straightened the bed until it was magazine-perfect again. Then she tucked the pocket watch back under the covers with her note pinched inside it. She took one last look at Katie's room before hurrying downstairs and zipping her coat against the cold.

With every step, Ana found herself longing to be home already. When she turned into her driveway, she paused to look up at her house. It wasn't like Katie's, and her life wasn't like Katie's, but *she wasn't Katie*. This was her home, filled with the people she loved most (plus Babushka) and the holiday that meant something to her family. Now that she'd seen again what a real family looked like, she could remember moments when her own family had almost gotten it right, and she felt surer than ever that they could make it happen again.

Pesky as he was, Katie would never have a Mikey, and suddenly Ana felt very sorry for that. The Burtons' lights might be more colorful, but it was the menorah lights that shone back at her from every December of her life. Hopefully she could help them light it tonight.

Ana hurried to her front door and turned the knob, ready to embrace it all and maybe even apologize, if that's what it took.

"You're late," said Ana's mom, as soon as she stepped inside.

"I'm sorry," Ana said, trying not to lose the feeling she'd had as she walked home. Why was it so much easier to love your family when they weren't around?

The light from the hallway cast sharp shadows across Babushka's weathered face. "You cannot always be sorry," she said. "What good is sorry when your family sits here in the dark? The menorah should have been lit hours ago."

Ana's mad was coming back fast. "I wasn't gone for hours, and you could have lit it without me," she said. "That's what we do, right? If somebody's not here, we just go on without them."

"Ana," warned her mom.

"Or we replace them with the Russian police," she muttered.

"Ana!" snapped her mom.

Babushka laughed. "I like that. Yes, I am Russian police. Tonight, police will report stolen property."

"What?" Ana and her mom asked together. Had Babushka finally figured out who had stolen the red socks from her knitting bag? That had been weeks ago.

Babushka scowled. "My suitcase is empty. Ana knows what should be inside."

Ana's stomach dropped. Had Katie *stolen* the watch?

It didn't matter. Ana was a loyal friend, not a rat.

"I know there was a watch in your suitcase, but I didn't steal it. That bird on the back is super creepy."

Babushka almost looked wounded, but then she sniffed and sat up straight. "The watch is made by hand in Russia. Not in factory full of American plastic. You do not like anything unless it is made of plastic."

Ana was sick of being insulted and accused. Maybe the reason they'd all been feeling rotten was because Babushka made everything seem that way.

"If Russia is so much better, why haven't you ever gone back there? If we're so awful, why are you still here?"

Babushka pointed a finger at Ana. "Because home is home. Family is family. Nothing is more important than this."

"Well you sure did a crappy job of teaching your son that."

Babushka clutched a hand to her stomach, then crumpled in her chair, like her bones had suddenly gone soft.

"That's enough!" Ana's mom slammed her hands against the coffee table so hard it shook. "Everybody, that's enough. I can't handle this."

With shaking hands, she lit the shamash, then lit all the other candles herself without saying a single one of the prayers. They all knew that was the wrong way to do it, but even Mikey knew not to say anything.

Ana's mom turned to them. "Just go to bed, everybody. Please." Nobody looked at each other as they left the candles to burn themselves out.

Upstairs, Ana locked her bedroom door and slid between the cold, stiff layers of her sheets. She wanted to get back to the feeling she'd had walking home. She wanted to live in the movie she'd seen in her head, of four faces smiling in the light of the candles with fresh latkes in everyone's hands.

Hanukkah was supposed to be about rebuilding. So why was everything falling apart?

Ana waited for a knock, a stern lecture, a list of chores for punishment, Mikey's little voice . . . anything. But soon, the house was silent, and she was still alone.

Katie

Chapter 15

THE MUSIC OF *The Nutcracker* wove its way through Katie's mind all the way home. She waltzed lazily into her room, ready to let the melodies and the memories of the night carry her right off to sleep. But when she clicked on her bedside lamp, something was different.

Ana's beanie still lay on the dresser, exactly as she'd left it. The same books still lined the shelves in neat rows, except for the small pile on her nightstand. Her closet was every bit as messy as it had been before.

Katie looked back toward her bed. She reached under the covers and was relieved to feel the cool weight of the watch against her fingers. But something else crackled inside it.

A note. Katie unfolded and began to read.

Dear Katie,

Your parents love you more than anything. That's so lucky. I'm sorry you got hurt, but I know you'll get better soon. I hope you still trust me, because I trust you. And I take back what I said before about you needing to find some courage. Just stay safe, okay? You're already brave.

Ana

As she folded the note back up, Katie wondered what kind of note Ana would have written if she knew the truth. Katie's parents did love her, and that was lucky, but what about the parents who had given her away?

And the part in the middle. *I hope you still trust me, because I trust you.*

Of course she trusted Ana. It hadn't been her fault Katie had fallen.

Except if she really trusted Ana, wouldn't she trust her with her secrets? Ana definitely wouldn't think Katie was brave if she knew Katie didn't even dare tell the truth.

Katie tucked the note into her nightstand for safekeeping. If Ana thought she was brave, she would be. Katie would tell her best friend everything the very next chance she got.

So first thing Monday morning, Katie got her mom's permission for Ana to come over after school.

"Of course," she said as she cut beef into stew-size strips for the Crock-Pot. "I didn't think she needed an invitation. Make sure she brings her little brother too. I don't want him alone in that big house."

Katie zipped up her coat and checked to make sure her headband still covered her wound. "Their grandma is staying there."

"Oh."

"They call her Babushka."

"Oh!" Katie's mother smoothed out her apron and glanced toward her little study.

"He can still come, though. I like Mikey."

Katie weighed her words the whole walk to school with Ana and Mikey, and when she got to the frost-covered playground she finally asked.

"Hey, after school, if you're not busy, maybe you guys could come over to . . ."

"Yes!" said Mikey. "We super could!"

"We'll come for sure," Ana said. "There's something I need to talk to you about, but it feels awkward to ask you here." Katie had never seen Ana so serious. "We'll be friends no matter what, but I need you to tell me the truth."

"Okay," Katie said. She felt a little sick as they walked to class. Had Ana already found out Katie's secrets? Was it too late for the truth to come from her first?

After last recess, Ms. Decker spread old magazines and colorful paper from the recycling box across the art table.

"Today," she said, "we'll be making presents for your families—picture frames. We'll take a picture of each of you to put inside, and you can give it to anybody you like." She held up a picture frame covered in colorful paper circles, and Katie's heart sang. There it was—the perfect gift for her parents! They'd love it, she knew, and they'd put it proudly on display. If she made them something pretty from paper circles, it could make up for what she'd written on her last Thankful. Katie would make hers even better than the example. She'd be the perfect daughter from now on. No more writing hurtful things, no more sneaking off to skate.

Ms. Decker showed them how to cut the paper into strips—almost like the Thankfuls—and fold each piece in half. After that, each strip was rolled around a toothpick until it made a small, bright circle, and each circle was glued onto the picture frame.

"While you work," Ms. Decker said, "I'm going to read you some Christmas stories . . ."

Ana cleared her throat.

". . . and Hanukkah stories, and as many others as we have time for. Don't you love all the cultural celebrations this time of year? I want you to notice how different these stories are, but also to look for all the things you can find that are the same." She smiled at the class. "Luckily, we have time for quite a few, because this project takes a while."

"Wait, seriously?" Ana asked. "We're just going to throw all the different stories together like that? It'll be like solyanka."

"What's solyanka?" Ms. Decker asked.

"It's a soup my grandma makes. It's every random thing she's got, all mixed together."

Ms. Decker nodded. "I like that. A mixture of all the stories that make us who we are. I guess maybe we're all a little bit solyanka, if you think about it."

Katie began cutting her paper strips. She planned out her patterns as Ms. Decker read, hoping to recognize herself in one of the stories. What were the ingredients in her soup? She wasn't sure anymore.

After a Hanukkah story and a Kwanzaa story, Ms. Decker gave them a break, and Katie was proud to realize that her picture frame was the farthest along and looked the neatest too. She could make things. At least she still knew that about herself.

"Only a little longer," said Ms. Decker when she called them back. "We can finish these up tomorrow. Make sure you have plenty of paper strips, though. You'll need to cover the whole thing." As she found her next story, Ana pointed to her own frame, which was a disaster.

"Somebody needs to put this thing out of its misery," she whispered with a roll of her eyes. Katie giggled at the joke, then felt guilty because her own frame looked so much better.

Ms. Decker waited for the class to settle back into their project, then cracked open an old book. "*The Gift of the Magi*," she read, "by O. Henry."

Something about the story—the words, the rhythm—reminded Katie of her dad. It seemed perfect in the beginning: Two people who loved each other very much, and Christmas time, and even a beautiful pocket watch. Katie couldn't help but feel this story was meant for her.

Then everything changed as the story continued, and a sickness grew in Katie's stomach. The husband sold his pocket watch to buy combs for his wife's hair; she bought a chain for that same watch with the money she'd gotten from selling her hair. All that sacrifice, all for nothing. All because they were trying to keep secrets, like Katie was now.

Between the words of the story, Katie heard the gentle *shush* of a paper coming uncoiled on her frame. She had barely glued it back down when another released. Katie panicked and looked around her, but everyone else's papers seemed to stick on the frame, just as they should. Even Ana's were staying put.

"No," she whispered as she coated another one with glue. "No, no, no. Please just stay."

More glue made it look worse, and still the coils came undone, faster than she could fix them.

"'White fingers pulled off the paper,'" read Ms. Decker. "'And then a cry of joy; and then a change to tears.'"

It doesn't matter, the story seemed to tell Katie through her struggle. *Even if it's Christmas, and you've given all you have to make things perfect, and you love each other more than anything—even then it can all go wrong. One big mistake can ruin everything.*

Katie stared down at her art, just waiting for the next piece to come undone. She needed air. She jumped to her feet, right in the middle of Ms. Decker's sentence. "May I be excused?" Her voice sounded strange and strangled, even to her.

Ms. Decker nodded and gave Katie such a kind smile she almost cried. She planned to head down the hall to splash some cool water on her face and take a few deep breaths. But her feet carried her straight past the bathroom, straight out the main doors, straight toward her house.

The wind cut through Katie's thin sweater. The fresh

air probably should have helped, but being out beneath the big, cold sky only seemed to make room for her fears to grow. She didn't even know who she was anymore. Was she the straight-A student or the girl who left school? The one who was totally honest or the one who told lies and kept secrets? The perfect daughter who always obeyed, or the rule breaker who nearly broke her head open and left schoool early?

Katie didn't know. Now that she'd messed up in such a big way, a little part of her whispered, *This is who you really are, and it's not good enough.*

The only thing Katie was sure of was that she didn't want to be alone. She ran up the steps and burst through the front door.

"Mom!"

Silence.

"Mom? Dad?"

The rhythmic rush and drip of the dishwasher was her only answer. She raced to the garage and found nothing but dirty, damp tire tracks. Even outside, the streets were deserted. Katie put her hands against the glass and stared, stared, stared, hoping to see one of her parents drive around the corner.

It wasn't supposed to feel like this. Only a few weeks ago, when Thanksgiving break had started, her mom had been here, waiting and wanting to be with her. Shouldn't she be here when Katie needed her most?

The clock in the kitchen struck three, which meant that down the street, the bell was ringing too. Soon after, a dim rumbling of voices started from the direction of the school and a sprinkling of bright coats appeared in the distance. Katie retreated to her room and tore off her headband. She tore off the Band-Aid too and didn't even bother to put on a new one. The scab was still jagged and dark, but it felt good to let it show for once. She was done lying and keeping secrets.

When she heard the back door creak open and the sounds of shuffling in the kitchen, Katie took a few deep breaths, then hurried down the stairs, ready to tell her mom everything.

But it was Ana and Mikey, standing in front of the pantry with stacks of cookies in their hands.

"Hey," said Ana. "I hope it's still okay that we came over." She nodded toward the door, where three backpacks and coats lay in a pile. "Ms. Decker gave me your stuff. She totally noticed you left early, by the way. She says you can finish your project tomorrow."

Ana took a big bite of snickerdoodle and nudged Mikey with her elbow. "Let's get some milk."

Katie grabbed glasses for them, but she let Ana pour since she still felt a little shaky. When Ana and Mikey had settled at the counter with their snack, Katie cleared her throat.

"Do you want to know why I left today?" she asked.

"I think I know," Ana said. "But tell me anyway."

"Well," Katie said, "my project was falling apart."

"It wasn't worse than mine," Ana said. "Trust me."

Katie blushed. She'd forgotten about that part. "It wasn't just that, though. It was something about that story. The one about the couple and the hair."

"That ending was the worst," Ana said through a mouthful of cookie. "It made me glad you said no when I offered to cut you some bangs the other day." Then she stared straight at Katie and swallowed hard. "Oh, right. The hair . . . and the *pocket watch*."

"Right," Katie said, unsure why Ana was so focused on the watch. "But I just . . ."

With a crash and a gush, Mikey's glass toppled and milk rushed into his lap.

"Don't cry don't cry don't cry," Ana chanted as she lunged for a dish towel. "Please, please, Mikey, don't cry."

Katie got a wet cloth, relieved that she didn't have to tell the truth quite yet. She helped Ana clean up the mess—first on the counter, and then on Mikey.

"I look like I had an accident," he said. "I look like a baby, and Jarek's going to make fun of me again."

Ana knelt down and looked Mikey straight in the face. "He's not going to see you. Nobody's hanging out by the pond today. It's too cold. And he's not ever going to make fun of you again. Remember the puck?"

Did Ana still think her puck was like a firebird feather? Katie wasn't sure, but Mikey's face brightened.

"Plus," Ana added, "I bet Katie has some old pants you can borrow."

Mikey was big for his age and Katie was small, so her old purple sweats fit him pretty well. She worried he'd hate the color, but he just grabbed them and ran into the bathroom to change. When he was settled down and playing with the round nesting dolls in the living room, Katie decided to try telling Ana her whole truth again.

"Okay, so I was going to tell you something."

"About the story with the pocket watch," Ana said.

"And why it was so hard for you to sit and listen."

"Yeah."

"I think I already know. If you just give it back, it won't be a big deal. I'll take the blame if she's mad."

Katie paused. "Wait, what?"

"The pocket watch," Ana said. She stared Katie straight in the eye. "I know you took it. Babushka knows it's gone, and she was super ticked. But if you give it back, I'll work it out so she finds it lying around and thinks she lost it. That's the good thing about having a grandma that's turning every corner of your house upside-down."

This wasn't going in the right direction at all. "I didn't steal Babushka's watch, Ana."

Ana stood, her voice harder now. "You did. I saw it in your room when you were at the ballet. I left a note inside it, remember?"

"I didn't steal it. I'm not a thief," Katie insisted. "I'm not a liar." Her stomach twisted. She couldn't believe she'd said those words. Not when the whole point of having Ana over today was to admit she'd lied to her. Katie couldn't look Ana in the eyes. How had things gone so seriously wrong, when all she'd wanted to do was fix them?

"I want you to trust me," she whispered.

"If you want people to trust you, you have to tell the truth." Ana's voice was almost desperate now. "Admit you're wrong and give the watch back! I'm willing to fix this for you, but not if you keep lying to me. Geez, I have to fix all Mikey's problems too, but at least he's honest!"

Katie stood and faced Ana. "I'm telling you the truth, and I'll prove it." She led Ana upstairs and pulled out the pocket watch. "This one's mine. Your grandma's doesn't have the little scratch right here."

Ana looked conflicted, but only for a second. "You could have scratched it."

"I didn't," Katie insisted. "And I'll show you exactly where I got it!" She hadn't planned on showing anybody the box in the attic, ever, but she had to prove to Ana— and to herself—that she could tell the truth.

"Here," she said to Mikey, handing him the watch. "You hold this, so Ana knows I'm not trying to steal it."

Katie dragged Ana up to the attic. "There's a whole box of stuff up here, and as soon as you see inside, you'll know the watch belongs there too."

Ana rolled her eyes. "If the watch belongs in the box, why was it in your bedroom?"

Katie hesitated. "It just was, okay?" What was the point

of telling the truth if nobody believed you? "You can trust me or not, but I promise, it came from this box."

But when they reached the spot where the box should have been, there was only an empty space, a square of dust-free floor.

"It was right there!" Katie said. "You can see where it used to be." She began frantically searching for the box's saggy sides and yellowed tape.

Katie was suddenly so mad at the world, but especially at her mom. How could she have taken away the only things that had brought Katie closer to knowing who she was?

"That un-dusty spot doesn't prove anything," Ana said. "That's probably from one of your mom's boxes for her ten thousand Christmas decorations."

Katie was so upset for so many reasons that the words came out without her even thinking about them.

"She's not really my mom." As soon as she'd said them, she stopped. "I didn't mean that."

"So you lied. Again."

Katie felt sick. "It's more complicated than that."

"Either you lied or you didn't, Katie, and I'm kind of getting sick of trying to tell the difference."

"Here's the truth," Katie said. "I didn't tell you all my secrets before." She closed her eyes and took the leap, praying it would help. "I'm adopted."

With her eyelids shut tight, Katie waited—for the sick feeling inside to go away, for Ana to respond, for *something*.

"I'm adopted," she said again, a little softer. She opened her eyes.

"So that's your excuse for stealing stuff and lying about it?" Ana shrugged. "I already knew you were adopted."

Katie backed away. "You already knew? How?"

"I heard your mom telling somebody when you first moved in. Everybody knows."

"Everybody knows?" Katie leaned against the wall and slumped to the floor. "Everybody?"

"Yeah, and nobody cares. What's the big deal? I don't care if you're adopted."

"I care," Katie said. "If you were really my best friend, you'd care too, because *I care*." She stared up at the ceiling to try to keep the tears in. She couldn't cry in front of Ana. Especially not right now. "If you really don't care," Katie said, her heart freezing in her chest, "then I think you should go."

Ana just stared for a second. "Okay, sure. That seems

like a good way to fix problems. Somebody should just leave, huh?" She took one more look around the attic. "If you find your mysterious box or think of anything else you want to tell me, let me know. Me and Mikey are going home."

Home.

Katie sat alone in the corner of the attic, wondering how this had ever felt like a magical place. She imagined the hands that had laid one brick on top of another, nailed one smooth board to another, so that she could sit here now. She imagined a hundred years of families who had lived in this house before her, big and old-fashioned and smiling. Shouldn't those stories be part of her story too?

We share something important, she would say to them. *Don't you think we could mean something to each other?*

But when she looked out the attic window and saw her best friend walking away without even glancing back, Katie knew the answer.

Ana

Chapter 16

ANA STARED AT the sidewalk as she and Mikey left, but she could feel Katie watching her from the attic window. Her best friend had stolen Babushka's watch, and then she'd lied about it. She'd kept secrets from Ana and lied about that too.

Of all the ways Ana's dad had broken their hearts, it was the lies that had hurt the worst. About coming to more games this season, and finally taking her on a road trip. About being there when they got home from the lake.

The bracelet itched at Ana's wrist from inside her coat. She couldn't trust Katie. Not anymore. Probably never again.

And was she seriously supposed to feel bad for Katie just because she was adopted? At least she had two parents she could count on. Ana had nobody right now. Not her parents, not Mikey, not her hockey friends, and definitely not Katie anymore.

With a creepy shiver, Ana realized that the most dependable person in her life was actually Babushka.

That was too depressing to think about. Ana dropped her backpack in the kitchen as Mikey ran ahead up the stairs. At least he'd ended up with her this time instead of with Katie. She drank a huge glass of water, gulp after gulp without even stopping for air, hoping it might fill the hollow places inside her.

In her bedroom, Ana shed her damp shoes and collapsed on top of her covers.

Then Mikey's little voice piped up from under the bed. "Ana, that was sad."

Ana rolled to the edge of the bed, belly down, and dangled her arm toward the floor. "Yeah, it was."

Pretty soon, Mikey reached out and laced his fingers in with hers.

"If you're sad now," he said, "that means we're all sad. Me, you, Mom." Mikey sniffled. "I have to fix it."

"That's not your job, buddy," she said. "That's my job." But when she said it, Ana realized how little she'd been doing lately to put her family back together.

Mikey let go of Ana's hand and began playing with her bracelet. "This is pretty. Katie has one too."

"I know," Ana said. "She made them." But could Ana even believe that anymore? Katie had lied about the watch and about telling her secrets, so she'd probably lied about other stuff.

Mikey twisted the bracelet. "Can I see it?" he asked.

"Go for it." Suddenly, Ana wanted to be rid of it. "Actually, could you give it back to her for me?" She felt Mikey's little fingers pulling the bracelet off, and then it was gone. When she closed her eyes, Ana could still feel the place where it had rested for the last three days.

Chik-chik. Chik-chik. Mikey tapped his lucky orange marbles together under the bed.

"I've been thinking about my superpower. I think I'm Pair Kid."

"Um, okay. What does that mean?"

"Like putting things in pairs. You know how I'm really good at that?"

"You are," Ana said. She couldn't bring herself to tell him that matching up shoes probably didn't count as a superpower. "But remember what they said to Spider-Man. 'With great power comes great responsibility.' You'd probably better pair those bracelets back up right now."

Mikey scrambled out from under the bed. "You're right! I'm on it, Ana. Pair Kid, power up!"

After Mikey had left to return the bracelet, Ana trudged back down to the kitchen, wishing it smelled like snickerdoodles. She picked up her backpack and pulled out her math book before she could get in trouble.

"Straight to homework," said Babushka, coming into the kitchen behind her. "Good girl."

Good girl. Ana could barely believe Babushka had spoken those words. "Um, thanks." They worked in silence, Babushka chopping cucumbers with an enormous knife, Ana working through one math problem after another. The kitchen didn't smell like Katie's, but after a while, it smelled like something spicy and savory instead that made Ana's mouth water.

Ana knew how to get the answers to her math home-work, but dividing fractions still seemed all wrong. If she divided by half, how did the bottom number get bigger? The whole world was fractions, she realized. Only parts of what should be whole.

Two-seventeenths of her problems done. That was a terrible fraction.

Three-fourths of a family. Even worse.

One-half of a best friend bracelet. But she didn't even have that anymore.

Ana plugged along until she'd reached nine-seventeenths of her problems done. Then a sound cut through the quiet of the kitchen. Shouting first, then sort of a scream.

"Did you hear that?"

Babushka tipped her head to the side as she stirred the soup. "I hear nothing."

Ana turned back to problem number ten. She under-stood how to get the answers, but she didn't understand *why*. It felt like cheating to write them down. Like taking something that didn't belong to her, and lying about it.

I bet Katie doesn't worry about that.

There was the sound again. This time: shout, other

shout, then a scream that was definitely Mikey.

Babushka turned toward the back door, but Ana beat her to it. She bolted outside and toward the terrible sounds. A gang of fifth graders stood at the edge of the pond, and between them she could see Mikey's skinny legs, flat against the snow.

"Hey," she yelled, racing toward them. "Hey!"

The boys stepped back, and Ana could see her brother clearly. A trickle of blood crept from his nose and down his chin. Ana rushed over and knelt behind Mikey.

"It's okay," she said, grabbing him under the armpits. "I've got you." His little body leaned into hers.

Ana glared up at the boys.

"Who did this?" she demanded. "Who hit him?"

Jarek stepped forward. Of course. She should have known it would be that weasel.

"Nobody hit him," Jarek said. "We were just messing around and he got a bloody nose. He's seriously that much of a pansy."

Ana pulled Mikey toward her, shielding him from the other boys. "If I ever hear that you talked to him, or touched him, or even breathed in his direction, I will flatten you." She heard the murmurs and snickers of Jarek's little gang, but she didn't care. She'd flatten them too, if she had to.

Jarek spat on the ground. "He was wearing a bracelet a minute ago! If he doesn't want to get picked on, maybe he shouldn't act like a girl."

Now Ana's blood throbbed in her head. "Tell me," Ana said. "How does a girl act?" She gave Mikey a little squeeze, then stood. Jarek had ten pounds on Ana, but after five years of hockey, she had no doubt she was tougher.

"Does a girl do this?" Ana stepped forward and flicked the side of his neck with her finger.

"I guess ugly girls do," said Jarek. His buddies laughed. "Did you know your brother plays with the girls at recess?"

Ana hadn't known, but when she was Mikey's age, she'd played basketball with the boys every recess. Nobody had cared. Was this different?

Maybe, she admitted. She wasn't sure.

But then she had to ask herself: Did it matter?

It only took one look at Mikey to answer that question. He had been walking along, wearing her bracelet, and *he had been happy.* The problem wasn't Mikey. The problem was bullies who were too stupid to make room for anything different in their tiny brains.

Jarek stepped up beside Ana and spat, missing Mikey by half an inch. "What do you expect, though? His parents are losers, so of course they have a loser kid." He kicked a skiff of snow toward Mikey.

"All I have to do is touch him and he'll start crying. Like a loser. Watch . . ."

Jarek reached the toe of his boot toward Mikey's shoulder and pushed him back to the ground. Mikey closed his eyes, but the tears still came, leaving tiny melted circles where they landed in the snow.

Something hot and fierce rose in Ana's gut.

"I warned you," she said, in a voice that barely seemed like her own.

Then Ana pushed Jarek, hard as she could, and he fell straight through the ice and into the pond.

Katie

Chapter 17

THE ATTIC FELT emptier than ever to Katie after Ana and Mikey left. No box. No best friend. No reassuring little hand in hers, like there had been last time she and Ana had argued. Mikey had even taken the watch, and Katie had let him. She didn't deserve it anyway.

Katie turned off the one dim bulb and shut the door behind her, and all her mistakes seemed to press her down, down, down as she descended the attic stairs. She'd kept so many truths from so many people she cared about that it was hard to imagine anybody would ever trust her again.

Katie sat in the cold draft from her window until a soft knock brought her from her thoughts. She took a deep breath.

"Come in."

Katie's mother opened the door awkwardly with a box against her hip. For a second, Katie hoped it could be *the* box, but the word "Christmas" was scrawled across the side.

"It's about time we finished decorating," her mom said. Then her eyes grew wide.

"Oh honey, what happened?" She dropped the box on the bed and rushed across the room.

Now Katie could tell her mom about Ana and her terrible day at school, and everything would get better somehow. But then she realized where her mom's eyes lingered—at the giant gash on Katie's forehead that she hadn't covered back up.

For a moment, Katie wanted to back out. She started thinking up a story, something about slipping on the way home from school. But she couldn't do it anymore. She was done lying.

"I fell. I checked the other box on the permission slip and went on the field trip and ice-skated and I fell." The words rushed out, and they brought her tears along with them. "I'm sorry, Mom. I'm so sorry."

Katie's mom stiffened for a second, but then she pulled her close. "I'm going to be very upset with you in a little while, but right now, I'm just glad you're okay." She pulled back and brushed the hair from Katie's forehead. "Oh, sweetheart. This looks terrible. I wish you had let me clean it before it scabbed over. I hope it doesn't get infected. Now do you see why you shouldn't do things like that?"

The word "yes" almost escaped Katie's lips, but her heart called the lie back. "No," she said. "I guess I don't. Anybody could have fallen. I didn't fall because of my heart."

Katie's mom folded her arms. "It was dangerous, and I had told you no. You're going to get me upset sooner than I thought."

Was it so awful if they got upset once in a while? Was it breaking a rule to be anything besides happy?

"Well, maybe I'm upset too," Katie said.

Katie's mom sighed. "I can see that," she said, her voice

cool but strained. "Now, settle down. I thought we could have a nice time decorating your room." She began lifting things out of the box, her mouth pulled into a thin line.

Now Katie didn't even have the right to get mad? She grabbed handfuls of her bedspread to keep herself from grabbing the box and throwing it out the door.

"Why can't you leave things in the attic?" The words came out louder than she'd meant them to.

"Why are you yelling?" Katie's mom frowned. "I thought you liked all the Christmas decorations."

Something inside Katie had freed itself, allowing her to say exactly what she was thinking, and it felt like pure hot electricity. "I'm not talking about Christmas decorations. I'm talking about the other box you took—the one with my stuff."

"I don't know what you mean," her mom said, unloading the contents of the Christmas box onto Katie's bed. "We took some things to charity like we do every year, but none of it was yours."

"Yes it was! How do you know it's not mine if you don't even ask?"

Katie had never shouted at her mom before, and they both stared for a moment. The strange current zipped through her, sharp and dangerous, and she turned away from her too-perfect mother and her too-perfect decorations.

Katie's mom picked up the emptied box. "I don't know what this is about, but I'm going to leave before you get yourself in any more trouble. Take all the time you need to settle down, but don't come out until you're ready to apologize."

The door clicked shut and her mom's footsteps faded. As Katie turned back to the now-empty room, the electricity left, and a hollow ache filled her chest. All she wanted to do was crawl into bed and fall asleep and wake up in a world where she knew who she was and who she wanted to be—and where those things were truly her choice.

But she couldn't even do the "crawl into bed" part. Her mom had left Christmas decorations all over it.

Katie sighed and looked over the decorations. The little wooden nativity had always been her favorite. She'd spent hours playing with it, telling herself the story of the tired mother and the small, new baby she loved more than anything.

"I will never leave you," her Mary had whispered to the little bundle in the manger. "Not ever. Not for anything."

But the story was too painful for Katie to tell this year. The whole point of Christmas was a birth story that millions of people had already known for thousands of years. *This is important*, all the songs and stories and symbols repeated. *The thing that matters is how and where you were born.*

But what if you didn't know? What if you could never know?

There was a soft knock on her door, and Katie brushed the tears from her eyes.

"I'm still upset," she warned. "You'd better not come in."

After a long pause, a little voice came from the hall. "Okay. I'm sorry."

Mikey?

Katie opened the door, and there he stood, smiling at her shyly like he was actually happy to see her.

"Sorry," Katie said. "I'm not upset at you. I thought you were someone else." She looked behind him, but Ana wasn't there.

"I'm just me," Mikey said. He held out the purple pants, all bunched up. "These are for you. Sorry I spilled."

"It's okay." The whole thing seemed like it had happened last week.

Mikey stepped forward and hugged Katie hard around

the waist. "We're fixing everything. Don't worry. Oh, and here." He pulled up his sleeve and handed Katie the other half of the best friend bracelet. "This is from Ana. I hope that makes it better. It's really pretty." Then he scrambled down the stairs and out of sight, and Katie was alone again.

Good, she thought, slipping the bracelet around her wrist and snapping the two halves back together. *Now I have them both again.*

But it didn't feel good. Not at all. Katie stared out the window and into the dull gray haze of the sky. She was sick to death of snow. How had it ever seemed magical when it was just cold and dirty? None of it was beautiful, not even the snowflakes. Especially not the snowflakes.

One by one, Katie ripped the paper snowflakes from the window. So crooked, so ugly. Why had she ever thought they were good enough? After the last one had been torn down, Katie stared at the bracelets and realized they were crooked and ugly too. She took hers off and fit the two halves together, then threw them onto the bed. She had wanted them both so badly, and now she'd gotten exactly what she deserved.

Katie wouldn't let herself look over at the nativity fig-ures on her nightstand, but she couldn't block the image from her mind. The mother, and the newborn baby she adored. The perfection of it tore her apart.

Katie didn't go down for dinner, even though the smell of stroganoff made her belly ache. When her dad brought a plate up, Katie nodded and thanked him but kept staring out the window.

"Your mom told me what happened. I suppose you're still in trouble," he said. "But whatever is going on with you, we can fix it."

Katie thought of the forged permission slip, the torn-up snowflakes, and the blank space in the attic where the box had been. Of the last link of the Thankful Chain and all the trouble it would cause—but how impossible it would be not to say those words after all this time.

"No," she said softly, telling herself not to cry. "I don't think it can be fixed."

Katie's dad kissed the top of her head, just above the gash. "Tell me when you're ready to talk about it."

I'm ready now, she thought. *Please stay.* But she couldn't make herself ask. Why had it been so much easier to speak when she was angry? She struggled to find any words that might keep him there a little longer.

"What happens at the end of *The Snow Child*?"

Katie's dad straightened his sweater. "Well, there are lots of different endings. My favorite is the one where she learns she's the granddaughter of the Russian Santa Claus and joins him in the frozen North."

It wasn't a terrible ending, but if that was his favorite, the others must be worse. "Does she stay with her parents in any of the stories?"

His eyes grew sad, but he only hesitated a moment. "She does in mine."

Katie told herself to look up the ending of the story the next morning, but she found she didn't want to know. She tried to tell herself she didn't need anybody, but the truth seemed to be that nobody needed her. She was the kind of kid you could do without. All week, the world went on as Katie disappeared, little by little, from her own life.

She woke up later and went to sleep earlier.

She ate a little less with every meal.

Ms. Decker didn't even notice that Katie never raised her hand or spoke a single word.

Ana never waited; she just hurried Mikey home after school. No candles shone in either of the girls' windows anymore.

Katie's mom spent more and more time in the little study at the back of the house, and her dad began to join her there. They never once asked Katie if she'd taken her medication. Not even Katie noticed her own heartbeat much anymore.

As the Thankful Chains grew shorter, they seemed to be counting down the days until Katie vanished completely.

Ana

Chapter 18

ANA'S HEART POUNDED as Jarek sat thrashing in the half-frozen pond. "Next time, it'll be worse," she yelled. "Don't even test me. Mikey is the best kid that ever lived, and you don't get to tell him there's one single thing wrong with him."

A stream of Russian cursing came toward them. Ana squinted into the sunlight as she turned to face Babushka, but Babushka marched right past her and straight into the pond. She picked Jarek up by the armpits, then spun him to face her.

"It is too cold for swimming," she said in a low, dangerous voice. "How stupid of you to fall in."

Ana ran back over to Mikey, but she couldn't stop staring at Babushka in the water with Jarek.

"I didn't fall!" Jarek pointed at Ana. "That ugly freak pushed me."

Babushka grabbed Jarek by the shoulders, his coat giving way like bread dough under her strong fingers. "Careful," she warned, "or you may fall in again." With that, she swung his shoulders toward the shore, and he stumbled out of the pond and onto the snow.

Babushka stood there, still knee-deep in the icy water, her long skirt pooling around her. She pointed and glared at each of the boys in turn. "You would all be wise to listen. Terrible things happen to terrible children, and the witch will be watching."

The boys gaped at each other, then took off running as Babushka stood there and cackled. Something inside Ana seemed to melt as she gawked at her grandma.

"That was amazing," she said.

"Of course," Babushka said. "Now pull me out. We will talk about your punishment when I can feel my feet again."

Ana steadied Babushka as she lurched out of the pond. They gathered Mikey and trudged up the hillside together in silence.

Inside, Ana shed her coat and shoes and headed upstairs for dry socks. But Mikey was already up there, staring at their mom's door.

"I wanted to tell her," he said. "But I think it's a bad day."

Ana couldn't argue with that. This had to be the worst day of her life.

No, she remembered. *There was a worse one last summer.*

But at least there had been three of them then. At least they had been able to curl up in their mom's bed and all cry together. She listened at the doorway, hoping for any sound she could use as an excuse to go inside.

Nothing. The room might have been empty, or her mom might have been in there. On the bad days, it didn't make much of a difference.

Ana put an arm around Mikey's shoulders and gently guided him toward her room. "You can talk to me instead." She tried to think of a good distraction. "Who are the Flyers playing today?"

"I don't know. I didn't check." Mikey panicked. "They need my good luck. Where are my marbles?"

"Hey, it's okay, Mikey. You go find them, and I'll check the schedule."

Ana meant to look, but a headline on the Flyers' website knocked the breath right out of her.

Two for One Trade: Flyers Gain Draft Picks, Petrov Leaves for Detroit

He was playing for the Red Wings now. He'd asked for a trade again, but this time, he hadn't even told them.

He'd been gone for months. So how did this feel like him leaving all over again?

With a sick shock, Ana realized what this meant for the plan she'd been too busy to keep planning. The Flyers were playing in the Winter Classic, not the Red Wings. The Red Wings only played in Boston a few times a year. Ana clicked over to the Bruins' schedule and bit her lip as she waited for it to load.

This Friday.

The Red Wings were coming to town just four days from now. After that, they wouldn't be back again for another month.

Ana paced the room. She'd thought there would be more time. She hadn't figured out any of the details yet, like how they'd get to the game or what, exactly, they'd do when they got there.

And now she only had four days.

Mikey came back, clacking his marbles together. "Who are they playing, Ana?"

"Detroit."

Mikey frowned. "Are you sure? I thought . . ."

"Detroit, buddy. He plays for Detroit now." She tapped her fingers against the tablet, not sure what to do next.

But then she knew. "Hey, Mikey? I need you to go get your paper chain."

Mikey ran to his room and came back with his paper chain and about a hundred questions. To answer him, Ana just ripped off the last ten links they'd added and drew a family of stick figures on the new last link.

"You had it right before, Mikey. We never needed those other links. This is the day we get Dad back." Ana said a prayer and floated a wish toward the puck, hoping for any help she could get. Go big or go home. Except "home" was exactly what she had to fix.

Go big, then. She had to believe in herself again, for all of their sakes.

"This is the day everything goes back to better."

All week, Ana planned and practiced, and Mikey even stayed out of her way.

On Tuesday, Ana counted up the money her dad had given her for every goal she'd scored last season. They'd never had to pay for tickets before, but according to the website, she had enough. (And according to the website, she never could have afforded the Winter Classic anyway. It was destiny for sure.)

Next, Ana dug through boxes in the basement. Finding her dad at the regular arena would make things a lot easier, because she'd grown up there—and because of Bruins Giving Back. Thanks to Markov and his youth-groups-at-home-games organization, she had a way to get past security and find her dad.

Ana rummaged around until she found a box with special Bruins jerseys that were just the right sizes. Okay, the jerseys wouldn't get them into the visitors' locker room, but they'd get them a whole lot closer than any plan she'd had for the Winter Classic. Ana could improvise the rest when they got there.

On Wednesday, Ana brought her picture-frame project home from school. She'd seen a box of old photos the day before, and she spent the afternoon hiding in the basement and looking through them, trying to find the perfect one to go in her frame.

Hockey team photos—hers and her dad's.

Formal family portraits where they all looked a little uncomfortable.

School pictures where she looked ridiculous. She really should let somebody fix her hair, at least once a year.

Ana searched for something better. Didn't anybody ever print the good ones? Or were they all lost on a cell phone or stuck in a computer somewhere? Ana didn't dare ask her mom.

But then, at the bottom of the box, Ana found an old photograph of all four of them at the Bruins' family carnival. Mikey held a paper cone of pink cotton candy, bigger than his head. He grinned up at Ana, and the rest of them smiled down at him like he'd just won the Stanley Cup. Nobody even looked at the camera because they were just so happy to be with each other.

That was the one. Ana fixed it into the frame.

On Thursday, Ana told Babushka she had a homework project to do at Katie's, then practiced the long walk to the T station and bought plenty of tickets. She even rode two stops toward downtown before she decided she'd gone far enough and turned around.

As the T rattled down the tracks and back toward home, Ana tried to work out what she'd say to her dad. Sure, she hoped he'd spot them in the crowd and pull them into his strong arms and none of them would have to say anything at all. But she'd better think of exactly the right words, just in case. The trouble was, she might only have a few seconds. How was she supposed to fix it all in only a few seconds?

On Friday, she realized how. She needed Katie. Katie, who always knew the right thing to say. Who had found a way to connect with Ana's mom, maybe the first time they'd ever spoken. Who had eased Mikey's fears by listening to him instead of trying to get rid of them with a magic puck. Who had used nothing but kind, hopeful words to make Ana feel like things could be okay a hundred times since they'd met. She almost reached for a candle right then to give the signal—not just because of the mission, but because she realized how much she missed her friend.

Ana still couldn't stay mad, and she hadn't really been mad at Katie for days. She'd just been too busy planning. Since Katie had never believed in the plan, it hadn't occurred to Ana to have her be part of it.

But now, Katie seemed like the missing piece. The link that would hold all this together. Ana turned that thought over in her mind as she emptied her coat pockets. The arena didn't allow anybody to bring bags and Ana didn't own a purse, so they couldn't take much. And they had to be ready to leave as soon as it got dark.

The puck went in her coat pocket first, then the extra T tickets Ana had bought and every single dollar she had. If they needed much else, it would have to go in Mikey's coat pockets, which were probably stuffed with junk already.

Sure enough, Mikey's right pocket was loaded with candy wrappers and rubber bands and crusty, wadded-up tissues. Because of that, Ana was extra careful when she reached into the left one. But when she closed her fingers around two small circles, Ana almost swore.

Babushka's pocket watch, and another one just like it. Katie's.

A wave of sickness washed over Ana. Katie had been telling the truth all along.

But even if she hadn't, *even if she hadn't,* how could Ana have let their friendship fall apart over a watch and a little lie? Especially considering how many lies Ana had told in the last few days. What kind of friend was she?

The kind who fixes things. If she could fix her family— and in spite of everything, she believed again that she could—then she could fix this. Maybe she could fix it all today.

She just had to apologize and give back the watch.

Katie would forgive her. Katie would know what to say. Katie would make it all work out. Ana didn't just believe in herself, but in her friend too.

Ana shoved everything they'd need into the pockets. There wasn't room to take the family picture, and suddenly, Ana realized it wasn't her dad who needed it. He'd have the real thing right there. So, ugly as it was, she left the frame she'd made on her mom's nightstand. Half the papers had come uncurled, but at least it had that great picture inside. There were glops of glue showing, but at least it showed how hard Ana was trying to do things right. At least they were all in this together tonight, in some small way.

She grabbed Mikey and snuck to the back door.

"Is it time?" he whispered. He slid his arms into the coat, but not before Ana noticed he'd slipped the very last link of the chain around his wrist like a bracelet.

"It's time," Ana said. "Actually, we're a little ahead of schedule, but we need to make one extra stop."

Ana and Mikey stole into the darkness and planted themselves outside Katie's house.

"Why can't we just go inside?" Mikey asked.

"Because I messed it up," Ana said. "And so did you." Ana held out the watches. "Mikey, whichever one is hers, you've got to give it back."

Mikey's face fell. "But they're a pair."

Ana hugged him close. "Not all pairs get to be together, buddy. Not all the time." She shivered, telling herself it wasn't a sign of what would happen tonight. It couldn't be.

"Come on," she said. Outside Katie's house, Ana scraped some frozen-together gravel from beside the sidewalk. She climbed the snow banked against Katie's fence. "Let's get my best friend back."

One by one, Ana threw the tiny stones at the dark rectangle of Katie's window, praying it wasn't too late.

Katie

Chapter 19

THE PEBBLES STRUCK Katie's windowpane one after another.

Tink.

Tunk.

Each time a stone collided with the glass, a shimmer of sound waves rippled from the spot, weaving through her room and off her bare, dark walls. Finally, enough of these

228

invisible waves found their way into Katie's ears to pull her from her shallow, dreamless sleep.

She opened her eyes, but she didn't turn on the lights. Now that she'd finally settled into being alone, it seemed like so much work to live any other way. Maybe whoever it was would just give up and go away.

But they didn't. The pebbles continued to strike the glass. Katie dragged herself from her bed and knelt on the window seat, straining to see who had woken her. The window itself had frozen shut, but with a great jerk, it groaned and swung, nearly sending her tumbling to the ground.

The latch had scraped Katie's hand, which at least made her feel *something*. She pressed her knuckles to her mouth as she looked down toward the yard.

There was Ana, staring up at her from the snowbank. Ana had never looked like that before—like she actually wanted somebody to tell her what to do. *Vulnerable.* Katie's mom used that word to describe her all the time, but it had never seemed like an Ana word until now.

Katie called down to her. "I thought you were mad at me."

"I was," Ana said. "I'm not now. Now I'm sorry." She nodded toward Mikey, who held up a small, silver circle in each of his hands.

The pocket watches.

"You were telling the truth," Ana said.

A small anger bit inside Katie. Of course she'd been telling the truth. But then she remembered how much she'd been holding back.

Ana squinted up at her. "Were you asleep? It's seven o'clock. On a Friday night."

Friday. Maybe Katie could stay in bed all day tomorrow. She thought of the warmth of her covers. How easy it was now, to fall asleep and float away from the whole world.

"I'm just tired," she said. "I'll see you guys later." And she shut the window before they could pull her back out into the cold. All this mess had started the night she'd gone with them to the pond. How had she ever thought she was built for brave things?

Katie's sheets had already cooled by the time she slipped back between them. But before she could even warm them back up, the bedroom door creaked open. Two figures stood silhouetted in the doorway, much too small to be her parents. She pulled the covers to her chin.

"Get up," Ana said. "Um, please." She turned on the lamp. "I'm sorry, okay? I'll say it a hundred times if you want, but we kind of have to go." She pressed something round and smooth into Katie's hand, and Katie felt her own heart begin to wake with the *chik-chok* of the watch pulsing into her palm.

"Go where?"

Ana had pulled jeans from Katie's dresser already and was digging through her sock drawer. "To TD Garden. The hockey arena. The game's about to start."

"I thought the game was outside. On New Year's Day. The Winter Wonderland or whatever."

"Change of plans," Ana said, tossing the socks to Katie and pulling a Bruins jersey from inside her coat. "Different team, different game. It's happening tonight." She dropped her voice. "Your parents don't exactly know we're in here, and they don't exactly know we're leaving. Hope that's okay."

Katie thought of her parents and how little they knew about her life anymore anyway. "That doesn't matter, but I didn't say I was going."

As she shut Katie's sock drawer, Ana spotted the

bracelets on top of the dresser. She split them apart and held one out to Katie. "I made a mistake. A big one. But that doesn't mean we give up on each other." Something caught in Ana's voice. "We need you. I need you."

There they were. The three words Katie had been longing to hear all week. She looked up, a little hope beginning to wake inside her, but she couldn't quite take the bracelet. Ana had walked away once. She could do it again.

Mikey slipped his little hand in hers. "I took the watch. I'm sorry too. Ana said if we said sorry, we could be like family again."

"I said maybe," Ana said. "Katie still gets to choose." She piled the clothes up and laid the bracelet on top, then patted Mikey on the back. "Come on, buddy. We'll wait outside five minutes, but after that, we have to go." She looked at Katie. "I hope you'll come. Holy flip, do I hope you'll come."

Then they were gone. Katie leaned back against her headboard, the pocket watch growing warm in her hand. She didn't even need to count as she felt her pulse quicken under the weight of Ana's choice. *Her* choice. The slim second hand circled once, twice. She closed her eyes and counted the time as it passed without her.

Three minutes. Her dad's footsteps below her, but only going to the bathroom.

Four. Back to his study. He wasn't coming up to see her after all.

As the second hand made its final sweep before her five minutes were up, Katie opened her eyes and studied her choices.

Jeans, jersey, socks, bracelet. A journey into bright lights toward somewhere she'd never been before—and probably shouldn't go.

Pajamas, sheets, blankets, bed. Dark and warm and safe.

And alone.

As the final seconds ticked away, Katie knew her choice. She threw back the covers that had held her down more and more each day and grabbed the pile of clothes instead. But first, she slipped on the bracelet.

"Wait," she whispered, hoping that somehow the sound would find its way to Ana's ears, or her heart. Hoping she wasn't too late. "I'm coming. I need you too."

Ana

Chapter 20

ANA LOOKED DOWN at the pocket watch, wishing the five minutes hadn't already passed.

"Come on, Mikey," she said. "The game's starting. We have to get down there."

In the shelter of the T station, Ana handed Mikey his ticket. "Just stick together and stay behind that couple. Not so close that they notice us, but close enough that we don't look like we're here by ourselves." Ana's gaze darted around the platform. "It's so much more crowded than when I practiced. Mikey, don't you dare let go of me."

But already, Ana had lost the couple they were going to follow. The ground beneath their feet vibrated as another train pulled away without them on it. None of this was working out how she'd planned it. None of it was working out at all.

Do you believe in yourself, Ana Petrova?

There were still moments when she wasn't so sure.

Mikey tugged on her coat sleeve. "Ana."

But she couldn't move.

"Ana," he insisted. "Look."

Ana scanned the platform and there, seeming a little lost but not at all afraid, was her best friend.

"Katie!" Ana pushed through the crowd, against the current, until she and Katie were face-to-face. "You came."

Katie's lips drew into a sad smile. "You needed me."

All the worry rushed out of Ana in one big breath. "You got that right." She handed Katie the third ticket. "Come on," she said. "We've got to catch the next one."

And they did. As the train rumbled toward the arena, Ana filled Katie in on her new plan. They poured from the train car with the rest of the crowd and rode the tide of Bruins fans all the way to the stadium.

The game had started already, so Ana had her pick of open ticket windows. "Three, please. Cheapest seats you've got."

The lady printed three tickets and took Ana's money. "Where are your parents, sweetheart?"

"Gotta go!" Ana said, grabbing the tickets off the counter. "Thanks!"

Inside the arena, the concourse stretched both ways, and Ana froze. She hadn't thought about this part. She hadn't thought about a lot of parts, probably.

"What are we going to do?" she muttered. "Where do we even start?"

"Well," Katie said. "Where's your dad?"

"He's on the bench, or on the ice. But there's no way security would let us down there."

Katie looked around. "And where do the BGB kids sit?"

Ana pointed to the left. "Behind the benches. But we don't want to sit there yet."

Katie nodded. "What if we sit in our own seats for a while and see what's empty, and then we sit a few sections away and keep an eye on the BGB section? When they leave for the tunnels, we'll slip in next to them."

"Yeah," Ana said, her pulse already slowing a little. "That will work."

They rode a long escalator up to the balcony and found their portal. And then, from one step to the next through the narrow gap in the concrete, it all hit Ana at once and stole the breath right from her.

The thickness of the air, which never felt quite right for hockey.

The smell of popcorn and pretzels and something like yeast.

The sound of the crowd, rising and falling together like waves.

She'd never seen the game from this high before, or from this far away.

This used to be my favorite place in the world. Ana looked down at the ice, where the aggression and attack of each play gave way to graceful gliding whenever there was a pause in the action. For years, Ana had imagined herself playing in an arena like this someday, helping earn a gold medal for Team USA. Quitting hockey had left a hole in her life that had been filling in over the last few weeks, but now it bled and ached all over again.

This used to be my dream.

She scanned the jerseys on the visitors' bench, and there it was.

PETROV.

His hair was longer now, but even by the way he tipped his face up to spray it with water, by the way he tapped his stick on the wall, she knew it was him. For the first time since he'd left, there was her dad, more than just pixels on a screen or a number on a roster. Her actual dad, now in a red jersey.

He used to be my hero.

The chirp of the whistle and the sudden attack of a face-off brought Ana back. The Bruins' left wing passed the puck to his center, and the center took off. The defenseman rushed in front of him, and they both surged forward. In a blur of black and red and white and gold, the play charged down the ice, fast and fierce.

Two periods passed that way, and Ana's mind shifted from hockey to her dad to the impossibility of the task in front of her as often as the puck switched possession. They moved closer to the BGB section, but Ana was so wrapped up in the game she barely noticed. When Mikey was hungry, Katie took him for a pretzel. When he had to go to the bathroom, Katie walked him out and guarded the stall. Ana could barely tear her eyes from the ice.

Until the BGB kids began to stir.

"Now," Katie whispered. "Ready or not, we have to go now." She tucked their coats under their seats and straightened Mikey's jersey. "Act exactly as excited as they are." She looked at Ana. "And try not to look quite so scared, if you can."

Ana, Katie, and Mikey blended in with the other kids, cool as the arena ice. Except for all the sweat beading up on the back of Ana's neck. She had never wished so hard to be invisible.

The group wound its way past the security guard and down into the staging area, past the locker room door and into the tunnel. "Okay," said a college-aged guy with a little too much energy. "This is where we'll line up. Remember, high fives and quick cheers only, and stay against the wall so they don't plow you over. They can't sign anything or stop to talk. As soon as they pass, we're back up to our seats, all together. Got it?"

Ana's mouth went dry. She was only guaranteed a few seconds in the wrong tunnel, but it was the best she'd been able to do. Right now, though, it was hard to believe it was

239

enough, even though she'd planned for this part.

She pulled the little notes from her pocket and handed one to Mikey. "High-five this to Markov if I miss, okay, buddy?"

There was a loud cheer from the locker room, then footsteps.

"Here they come," said the guy. "Step back."

As if they sensed their team, the crowd began to roar, and the kids in the tunnel cheered even louder. Mikey plugged his ears, and by the time Ana was ready, the players were already rushing past. But not Markov yet. Right?

Right. There he was, dropping his shoulders and rolling his neck. He always got to come out last, Ana remembered, because these were his kids.

We were his kids, she thought.

And he thought so too. When Markov spotted them, his face lit up. He rushed forward and pulled Ana and Mikey against his pads. "I miss you," he said. Tears stung Ana's eyes. It was already so much more than she should have hoped for, but so far from enough.

Ana knew in that instant she had to choose between "I miss you too" and what she'd actually come here to say, to do. She couldn't feel it all at once.

She tucked the note into his glove. "Can you give this to him?" she asked. "I don't know how. But tell him we'll be in the old training room after the third period."

Markov nodded, and the coach bellowed at him down the tunnel.

Then he was gone.

Ana thought she might be sick. "We can't go back up there," she whispered. "Katie, please. I forgot to plan this part, but we have to stay down here somehow."

Katie just nodded. They stepped in line with the group, but when they reached a corner, she grabbed Ana and Mikey's arms and pulled them back. "Here," she said, and they ducked behind a cart full of folding chairs.

"What's next?" Katie asked, once they'd caught their breath.

Ana thought for a second. "We have to get to the old training room. It's going to be remodeled into a players' lounge, so it should be empty. But I'm betting there's still a monitor in there."

"How are we supposed to sneak all the way to the old training room?" Mikey asked.

Katie thought for a second. "We're not," she said. "If you're sneaking around, they always ask questions. Just act like you belong and everybody will think you do." Now Ana only had to come up with half the answers. She wanted to cry with relief that Katie was here.

So they strolled to the old training room like it was their own front door. They hardly saw a soul, and the few people they did see were way too busy to worry about somebody else's kids. With the training room door safely shut behind them, they settled in to watch the rest of the third period on a monitor in the corner.

When the clock ran out, it should have been the end of the game, but the score was still tied. Ana hadn't planned on overtime.

Still, if Markov had given her dad the note, he could be coming any second. She'd said "after the third period," not "after the game," and Markov was always so careful with his words. There was only a short break before overtime— not even enough time to smooth the ice. But enough time to walk down the tunnel. He had to come.

Ana watched the seconds tick down until overtime would start. He had to come he had to come he had to come he had to come.

She didn't give up until the puck dropped.

He hadn't come.

"So this is overtime?" Katie asked.

Ana swallowed hard. "Sudden death. They set the clock for five more minutes, but if anybody scores, it's over. If nobody scores, they have a shootout."

"And then what?" Mikey asked. "Ana, what do we do next?"

Ana dropped her head into her hands. A sinking, sick feeling inside told her he probably wasn't coming after the game either. "Can't it be your turn to figure out the next move?" she muttered. She felt the gentle weight of Katie's arm around her.

"Maybe he'll come," she said. "Let's wait and watch. He might give you a signal or something."

Ana tilted her face toward the screen, wanting to believe that Katie could be right. That she had been right all along, and everything would be okay somehow.

After three incredible saves by the Red Wings' goalie, the play shifted. Ana's dad poised himself at the wall, ready to go onto the ice. Then seamlessly, the line changed and his turn had come.

Somehow, Ana knew what would happen even as the

play was unfolding. *He'll be in position right on time. The center's their best scorer, so the defense will cheat away, and he'll have an open look.*

Just as she'd predicted, the defense cheated toward the center, and her dad was left wide open. Even the goalie wasn't paying any attention to him.

Nobody's worried about him at all. He's only been gone half a season, and the Bruins have already forgotten how good he used to be.

But his teammate knew. He sent a perfect, whip-quick pass between the defenders. Even as her dad wound up for the one-timer, Ana couldn't decide if she *wanted* him to score the goal, if she wanted him to win the game, but she knew he would.

The rubber hit the back of the net, and the horn blared, and Ana couldn't help it—she was proud of him.

But only for a second. As the team rushed onto the ice to celebrate, something else caught her eye from the corner of the screen.

Somebody small was following them out onto the ice.

Mikey.

Ana

Chapter 21

MIKEY HAD NEVER looked so small—a dot of color against all that white, barely half the height of the players on their skates. The Bruins and the refs saw him right away and started toward him, but the Red Wings were too busy celebrating to pay any attention.

"STOP!" Ana screamed at the screen, but over the blare of the goal horn, she barely heard herself.

In the terrible space of half a second, the Red Wings

split apart and sprinted for their bench with their eyes on the scoreboard, and the crush of their bodies hit Mikey with the force of a freight train. His little body slid across the ice and into the boards, and finally, *finally,* the skaters were still.

Ana tore her gaze from the monitor and raced for the tunnel, where a guard waited.

"Please," she begged as Katie caught up. "There's a kid on the ice. He's my little brother." She tugged at the guard's radio. "Just ask. They'll tell you. We have to get out there."

"Ana," said a voice from behind the guard.

Markov.

The guard turned and startled.

"Let them come," Markov said. "Quickly."

They followed him through the tunnel and out onto the ice. Ana shoe-skated across and pushed her way between the massive bodies to the center of the hovering circle.

Mikey wasn't bruised or bleeding; none of his limbs stuck out at impossible angles. But Ana was almost sick to see him lying so still and gray. The medics were already all over him, calling for a smaller brace to strap around his neck and barking at the crowd to stand back. Ana held Mikey's hand as they loaded him onto the stretcher and wouldn't let go even when the crowd parted and they began to move toward the ambulance.

Then she felt a hand on her own shoulder. Markov again. "Ana, I'm so sorry. I did not see him." He wiped his eyes with the sleeve of his jersey.

"I know," she said. "It's not your fault."

"I told him to come," Markov said. "I gave him the message."

Her dad stepped up beside Markov, taller in his skates, huge in his pads, fierce with his bruised and broken face. The edges of Ana's vision blurred, and something white and hot burned in her belly.

"It's not your fault," she said again, straight to Markov. "It's his. This is all *his* fault. I don't know why I ever thought he could fix anything. He won't even walk down the hall when he knows we're right there." She snapped her head just enough to stare her dad in the face.

"I couldn't leave . . ." he started.

"All you do is leave!" Ana said. "You left us, you left Boston, and now you even left Philadelphia."

"Ana," he said. "I'm here now. I'll come with you."

Ana stepped between her dad and Mikey. "No. You

won't." She brushed the tears from her eyes. "I was proud of you for a second tonight. I hate myself for it now, but I was proud of you. You won the game. What more could you want?"

They both knew the answer to that. His family. He could want his family. He looked away, and Ana knew he didn't want it quite enough.

"Stay and celebrate with your team," she said. "Don't you dare come with us."

Ana raced to the tunnel where the stretcher was being loaded, grateful that Katie had stayed with Mikey every second. Katie climbed in the ambulance, then reached out and pulled Ana up.

"Excuse me, miss, but I'll need to . . ."

"We're family," Katie said, and the way she said it, the driver could only nod. They'd barely squatted down when the doors slammed shut and the siren started.

A paramedic pointed at the farthest corner from Mikey as the ambulance rumbled forward. "We've got to work, which means you've got to stay out of the way. You can speak, quietly and calmly. If he can hear you, it might help."

But Ana had no clue what to say. Would Mikey even

hear her, with the oxygen mask over his face and the brace around his neck? She wished more than anything she could hold his hand, but there were straps around his arms, binding him to the stretcher. Just then, she felt Katie's warm hand in hers. Almost like she'd heard the wish and knew the next best thing.

The two paramedics spoke in clipped, exact voices, fixing a tight band around Mikey's arm and a silver needle into his forearm. After a minute, Mikey seemed to move.

No, he definitely moved. Under the mask, he licked his lips.

Ana scrambled to Mikey's side, trying to make herself as small as possible so she wouldn't be in the way. So she wouldn't have to leave him. She knew he would hate this, but he had to wake up.

"Hey, buddy. Are you okay?"

The paramedic took off the oxygen mask, and Mikey coughed, sad and weak. "I think I'm not."

Ana nodded. "Yeah, I think you're right. But you will be."

"Did I get it?"

"Get what?"

"The puck. We only have one, Ana. That's why it only

works sometimes, for small wishes. A pair would be better. When he didn't come down, I knew he'd score a goal so I could have a pair." He looked straight into Ana's eyes. "Did I get it? Does it have the *M* scratches?"

"Oh, Mikey." This was all Ana's fault. But if she told him the truth about the puck now, it'd be like telling him he'd done this crazy brave thing and gotten himself in this mess for nothing. "We couldn't bring it right away, but we'll get it."

"Are we going home?" he asked.

If anybody said the word "hospital," Mikey was bound to freak out, but Ana was a little worried he hadn't realized he was in an ambulance.

"We can't go home yet," Ana admitted. "We've got to fix you up a little first."

One of the paramedics pushed her fingers into Mikey's belly. "It's rigid," she said. "He's got a bleed."

Ana was actually surprised by how little blood she could see on Mikey—mostly scrapes and scratches on his face, so small she hadn't seen them before, and nothing like when Katie had fallen. But the way the paramedics looked at each other, she knew this was bad news.

"Call ahead and tell them he'll need surgery."

That did it. A switch flipped in Mikey, and he looked around like a wild animal.

"NO!" he begged. "No surgery! I'll die if they cut me open!" He strained against the straps that held him down. "What are you doing to me? Where's the door? Let me out of here!"

The paramedics kept shouting numbers at each other, and Ana squeezed his hand. But Mikey had started to sweat, and an alarm blared from one of the machines.

"His blood pressure's way too low." The woman with the ice-blue eyes turned to the driver as her partner attached a tube to the needle in Mikey's hand. "Seriously, can't we go any faster?"

"Three minutes," said the driver.

"NO!" Mikey screamed again. But his voice was already weaker, and he seemed to drift away for a long moment before he remembered his fight. "Let me out! No hospital. No surgery. My mom's not here and you can't do anything if I say no."

Ana wasn't sure if that was true, but she worried it could be. She felt Katie's hand in hers again, this time pulling her away from her brother.

"He needs me," Ana pleaded.

"He does," Katie agreed. "But he might need me too, just for a minute." She squeezed herself into the spot where Ana had been and softly placed her hands on the sides of Mikey's face.

"Hey," she said, steady as the snowfall. "I need to tell you a secret."

Katie

Chapter 22

THE AMBULANCE WAILED and the stinging scent of something chemical snuck inside Katie with every breath.

"Mikey," she said, pushing her own fears and memories aside. "You don't have to have surgery."

The paramedics tried to argue, but Katie shook her head. Finally, Mikey settled down enough to look right at Katie. "I don't have to?"

"You get to choose." That was important. Mikey

needed to know it was his life, his choice. "But can I tell you another secret?"

Mikey nodded, and Katie leaned closer. It wasn't hard at all to tell her secrets now.

"Surgery makes you stronger."

Mikey's eyes filled with tears. "You don't know that."

"I do." Katie pulled down the collar of her shirt, just far enough for Mikey to see the bumpy pink scar. "I had surgery when I was little. Huge surgery. They gave me a new heart."

"Almost there," called the driver.

Mikey clutched Katie's hand a little tighter. "Were you scared?"

"I was so little I didn't even know it was happening. But if I had, I bet I wouldn't have been as brave as you."

Mikey loosened his grip, just a little. "It made you stronger? Like a superpower?" The words were a struggle now, and just breathing seemed to be taking his strength.

Katie leaned closer. "Shhh, Mikey. I told you, it's a secret. But it made me way stronger than I'd ever been. So yeah, kind of like a superpower. You go to sleep your regular self, and you wake up different. It won't feel super right away, but it'll come."

As the ambulance made a quick turn, Mikey let go.

"Okay," he said, in a strange, scratchy voice. "Okay."

Katie smiled at him. "You can do this. And you can show me your scar when it's all done."

The ambulance jerked to a stop, and a whole crew was waiting when the doors opened.

"If you get scared, just think how strong you'll be," she said.

As he slid away into the night, Katie thought she heard Mikey say, "Strong like you." She caught hold of the words, wanting him to be right for both their sakes.

Katie followed Ana into a waiting room, where a nurse let them call their families and promised that Mikey was in great hands. Once they were alone with the quiet tick of the yellowed clock above them, Katie couldn't help but remember how broken she'd felt only a few hours ago. Like she could just close her eyes and dissolve into the winter air.

But now she felt the seams and cracks beginning to patch together again. She fingered the friendship bracelet in her pocket, remembering how many of those cracks had formed between her and Ana. Of course she'd forgiven Ana for the watch, but had Ana forgiven her for everything else? Or had she just needed her help?

Ana stared straight ahead. "You told him he'd have a superpower."

Had she? Katie buried her head in her hands. How could she have lied again already? Of course Ana had heard everything in the ambulance.

Ana sniffled. "I think you're the one with the superpower."

Katie was too surprised to answer. All her life, she'd been the weak one, the slow one, the one who could barely breathe. Now that they were safe, she was totally exhausted. That sure didn't seem like somebody who had superpowers.

Except that when Katie looked at all she'd been through—the cold, the running, the impossible situations—she saw a different picture of herself. She'd made it through all that, and she was fine. Maybe better than fine. She'd made a difference to Mikey.

Ana paced in front of her. "What if you hadn't gotten us on the ambulance and he'd been in there alone? What if you hadn't been there to tell him it would be okay, and he'd gone into surgery thinking he was going to die?"

Katie patted the empty chair next to her so Ana would know she could sit down. "I'm glad I could help. Everything really is going to be okay." It felt like the truth too—not only for Mikey, but for all of them.

Then there were Katie's parents, dashing through the doors, gazes darting around the room until they landed on her. They'd brought Babushka and Ana's mom, too, looking less like a ghost than before. Everyone hugged and cried like they were all part of the same family. They all told each other the pieces of the story they knew.

Ana's mom pulled Katie close. "Thank you for being there for them." The soft tap of a teardrop landed on Katie's head. "Not just today." Katie hugged her back, thinking again how much smaller Ana's mom felt than her own mother.

"You have two good kids," Katie said. "You're a lucky family."

But so are we, she thought as she looked toward her own parents, clutching each other with tears in their eyes.

A doctor called Ana's mom away, and Katie's parents offered to help Babushka fill out paperwork, so Ana and Katie were left alone again.

Ana slumped in her chair. "I know I'm not the greatest planner, but I never thought it would all turn out like this. Holy flip, what a mess."

"I'm sorry he didn't come," Katie said.

Ana rolled her eyes. "I'm sorry I thought he would." She paused. "No, that's not true. I'm glad I saw him. He's my dad. He's half the reason I'm here, you know?"

Katie knew just what it felt like to long to see the people who'd given you life. She swallowed her own ache and followed Ana's gaze to where Ana's mom talked with the doctor in the corner.

"She's the other half," Katie said, and Ana nodded. Katie remembered how sad and alone she'd been earlier tonight. Was that how Ana's mom had felt all these months?

Then Katie wondered if Ana was right—if she really did know just the right words to say sometimes. The words inside her now felt heavy and important.

"Your mom needs you to need her right now. I know you're tough, but she'll just keep floating farther away unless she can feel that. You should tell her."

Ana nodded. "We do need her. I was afraid to tell her,

I guess. But I will. I know it won't get better if we don't say the things we're afraid of saying."

Katie thought of the things she'd been afraid to say ever since she met Ana. She pulled her hand back and tugged down the collar of her shirt again. When she showed the scar to Ana, it did seem like something that made her stronger. "I've been keeping other secrets, but I'm ready to tell you now. I'm sorry I lied before."

Then Katie told Ana everything about her heart and her history. They compared the two matching pocket watches as Babushka brought them steaming cider from the cafeteria.

"And where did your watch come from?" Babushka asked.

Katie thought of all the possible answers to that question. From her attic. From Russia, apparently. But how did it get from one spot to the other? And what was the story behind the rest of the things in the box? There was a hollow place inside Katie as she wondered where the other treasures might be now.

"I'm not sure where my watch came from," she admitted.

"It doesn't matter," said Ana. "Well, I mean, it does,

but . . ." She bit her lip. "It does matter. And I'm sorry I said I don't care if you're adopted. If you want me to care, I'll care."

Katie thought about that for a minute. "Thanks," she said. "I don't care that your dad left, unless you want me to."

Babushka reached out and put her hand to Ana's hair.

"I know," Ana said. "It's still a mess. It's always a mess."

Babushka pulled an old wooden comb from her bag and pointed it at the ground before her. Katie expected Ana to argue, but she just pulled the elastic from her ponytail and knelt down. "Could you do a French braid?"

Babushka huffed. "I will do a Russian braid." She nodded toward Katie. "This girl has a strong heart," she said. "But she needs to learn more of her country, like you."

One pull at a time, Babushka worked through all the knots until the comb slid through it, smooth and straight. Babushka hummed something soft and almost familiar as she braided, and by the time she'd finished, Ana could barely keep her eyes open.

"Good girl," Babushka said, guiding Ana's head to her lap. "It was a brave quest, but you rest now. The morning is wiser than the evening."

Ana's whole body seemed to relax, and she finally let her eyes close as Babushka stroked her hair. It looked so perfect and comfortable that it made Katie long for her mother. She looked toward the corner where her parents sat, almost dozing themselves.

"Mom," she said. "I'm ready to go home now."

Katie's family walked together to the parking lot. "You did a good thing tonight," said her mom as they buckled up, and Katie's heart swelled.

But then.

"You did a good thing, but a dangerous thing. You can't ever put yourself at risk like that again." She glanced at Katie in the rearview mirror, like she couldn't even bear to really look at her daughter. "Now let's get you home and in bed."

No. That was the last thing she needed. She'd been in bed too much since Monday, and she didn't ever want to feel that way again.

Katie reached forward and touched her mom's elbow before she could turn the key.

"I need to tell you something." Now her mom twisted

to face her, and Katie took a deep breath. She touched her fingers to the scar on her chest, hoping it would give her courage too.

"I've been so lonely and sad all week, and in the end, Ana was the one who was there for me. So I had to be there for her." Before her mom could argue, Katie kept going.

"You're right, though. I promise I won't sneak away like that again. But you're right about something else too: I did something good tonight. I made a difference for Mikey and Ana. For their whole family." She felt the truth of those words melting a hard place inside her. "Ana thought it was like a superpower. And you guys have always made me feel like there are super things about me, but it's the first time I've ever felt the *power* part. Like there's something strong inside me, and I really can do great things."

Katie's dad reached back and put a hand on her knee. "Of course you can." He looked to Katie's mom. "Can't she?"

"It scares me," she said in a small voice.

Katie tucked her hands underneath her legs. "It scares me too. I think it's supposed to."

"But what if we lost you?"

"You could," Katie admitted. "And I could lose you. But we still have to use our superpowers, don't we?"

They spent the rest of the ride home in a thoughtful sort of quiet. For the first time, Katie felt like her parents had truly listened. Like her words had power too.

Katie

Chapter 23

THE VERY NEXT night was Christmas Eve, and Katie had barely seen her mom all day. Instead of spending hours in the kitchen like she usually did on holidays, her mom had shut herself in her little study again.

"She's finishing up one last project," her father explained. "She's been working like this all week, hasn't she?" He glanced around at the cluttered counters, the bare stovetop, the empty oven. "How about hamburgers and root beer floats for dinner?"

Katie almost laughed. "For Christmas Eve?"

"Why not?" he asked, and Katie couldn't think of a single reason.

Katie lined up the fixings while her dad grilled, and her mom hugged them both close when she saw what they'd done. "What a wonderful new tradition," she said, and they all agreed.

After dinner, it was time to open the last link of the Thankful Chains. Katie's parents went first, both of them thankful for their little family. When Katie stood up to take down her last paper link, she stopped, knowing the time had finally come to read the words she'd written at Thanksgiving. She didn't want to hurt her parents, but this was something she had to say. Even if it made her belly flutter.

"I wrote something different this year," she said. "I hope it's okay."

Her parents smiled and nodded at her, and Katie ripped the link open and read the words, as if she couldn't be blamed for them if she were just reciting what was on the paper.

"I'm thankful for my birth parents."

Tears flooded her eyes, and when she looked up, her

mom was crying too. Katie dropped the paper and ran to her parents, desperate to fix it before she ruined everything. She searched her mind for the right thing to say, the best way to take it back. She buried her head in her mom's shoulder, but soon she felt a gentle nudge, and she lifted her chin enough to look up.

Katie's mom smoothed the hair from her face.

"Oh, Katie," she said with a tearful smile. "I'm thankful for your birth parents every day."

A warm wave of relief washed over Katie. "Really?" she asked.

"Really," her parents said together.

"Could we talk about them sometimes?" she asked. "Would that be okay? Even if we don't really know anything?"

"Of course," said her mom, pulling her closer.

"Of course," said her dad. "But I think we can do even better than that." He flashed Katie a wink. "I think this might be a good moment to open a present or two."

Each of Katie's parents chose a present from under the tree and sat next to her on the couch. Her dad handed Katie his gift first, square but not too heavy, wrapped in shiny red.

"Go ahead," he urged.

Katie carefully slid her finger under each piece of tape and unfolded the wrapping. Once the paper was gone, she knew the box, and she couldn't believe she hadn't recognized it before, even under the wrapping paper. With trembling hands, she pulled away the crackly old packing tape and opened the flaps to see the attic treasures she'd thought were gone for good.

Katie's gaze and her fingers floated from one to the next—the candlesticks, the nutcracker, the nesting dolls. They were all there.

"I thought I'd be surprising you with those," said her dad. "But your mother tells me you found them already. She said you noticed they were gone, and she set my mind at ease about the missing pocket watch."

Katie nodded, but she couldn't make herself look away.

"Remember the story I told you of when we met?" her dad asked. "Well, I bought an extra suitcase so I could bring things back for you. There were women at a market in the square, right next to the orphanage. They had little stands where they sold such beautiful things, so I bought one from each of them."

Katie thought she saw the women then—faint,

flickering pictures at the edges of her memory. They spread their brightly colored treasures under a blue Russian sky, and her birth mother sang as she set out her own stand. They bought small red apples and sat at the edge of the market so her mother could carve long curves of apple skin for her to gnaw on.

The picture changed as Katie imagined her dad there, younger and smiling, trying to speak the few Russian words he knew. She imagined the women laughing and correcting him in voices that were almost like Babushka's. But now when she pictured their faces, she realized they looked a little like her own.

"One from each of them?" Katie wondered if one of those women really could have been her birth mother. If maybe she had sold things at the market too.

"That's right," said her father. And the way he looked at her, she knew he had wondered the same thing. "We can get you a chain for that watch, if you want, so you can wear it around your neck."

Katie could almost see it then: playing with her mother's braid long ago, but also something smaller when she leaned forward. Had her mother worn a watch around her neck? It might be a memory. Another new first memory, hazy and distant, but real all the same.

Katie's mom knelt beside her and handed her the second package, longer and thinner and even lighter. Once again, Katie blinked in surprise after she'd peeled back the wrapping and lifted the lid.

Instead of the fluffy, fuzzy Christmas pajamas she'd expected, the box held a linen nightdress. The soft white fabric was embroidered at the collar and hem with delicate swirls and snowflakes, but still, it reminded Katie of the pattern on the pocket watch.

"I've spent the last week learning to do this for you," said her mom.

Katie looked up. "Who taught you?"

"Ana's grandmother." Katie's mom smiled. "Babushka. As soon as you said that name, I went right over. She's been helping me while you've been at school."

When Katie held the nightdress to her chest, she saw what had been hidden underneath the fabric: a journal with a red leather cover and two words embossed on the front:

My Story.

Katie opened the cover to find thick, creamy paper. Her baby picture—the only one she had—was there on the first page. She started to turn the page, but her dad reached for the picture first and pulled it from the four black corners that held it in place. "It was always stuck inside that frame before," he said. "Did you ever see the other side?"

Katie turned the photo over and there, below a line of Russian lettering in faded pencil, were the same swirled initials from the bottom of the matryoshka dolls.

She held them next to each other, then looked up at her dad, who gave her a sad smile and a small shrug.

They matched. Katie just knew it. She looked at the line of Russian words above. "Do you know what it says?"

"Babushka read it for us. 'Katya is a good girl,'" her dad recited, pointing at the words. "'A happy girl.'"

Katya. Katie had forgotten that used to be her name. She repeated the words, touching each one gently as a butterfly. Somehow, knowing that she had been happy then made it okay to be happy now, even with all the unknowns behind her and before her. She hoped her birth mom had figured out how to be happy too, but the hope was bittersweet.

Katie turned through page after page in her parents' handwriting. Her mom's neat, straight letters, and her dad's angled cursive.

"It's every detail we could remember about going to get you," her dad said. "And everything we know about what might have happened before."

Near the back, Katie found more pages in a scratchy scrawl she didn't recognize, and pictures sketched out in black ink.

"Who did this part?" she asked.

Katie's mom smiled. "That was Babushka too. She knows the village where you were born. She wrote down everything she could remember about it, and so many more things about the country you came from." She reached over and gave Katie's hand a squeeze. "She can't wait to talk to you about it."

Katie traced her fingers over the cobbled streets in the sketch and over the tops of the mountains. She studied the little houses and wished she could see inside their windows.

"Could you take me there someday?"

"Of course," said her dad.

"Whenever you're ready," said her mom. "Babushka says your favorite figure skater is from a village nearby."

Katie pictured Elena Korsikova doing beautiful, amazing, impossible things. They had something in common—something big. Maybe she could do beautiful, amazing, impossible things too, even if she never learned to quadruple toe loop.

When she'd changed into the nightdress and brushed her teeth, Katie snuggled under her covers. In her window, new paper snowflakes caught the glow of the lights that framed her window and encircled her miniature tree. Beside her bed, the little nativity rested.

Katie studied the small, wooden figures and thought of the baby born long ago in such a simple place. Maybe the story meant something different than she'd thought. Maybe people loved it so much because it didn't matter how you started out—not really. You could be anything you wanted, even if you were born in a barn or in a hospital halfway around the world. What mattered was what you did with the rest of your life. And how you helped people.

Katie's gaze drifted back out the window, where small, white flakes danced past. As much as she'd always loved Christmas morning, she might like Christmas Eve even more, because so many wonderful things were waiting ahead.

Because every story has a beginning, she remembered as she pulled the covers close around her. *And the rest of my story can be whatever I want it to be.*

Ana

Chapter 24

ON NEW YEAR'S Day, the sun slanted through Ana's window so bright and cheerful that she couldn't even be mad about being woken up. She pushed back the covers and shuffled over to look out at the clear, snow-covered world below. Another perfect day for ice-skating.

Katie had gotten new skates for Christmas, and they'd gone every day since. They weren't hockey skates, but Ana figured they had plenty of time to work up to that. One

274

afternoon, they'd caught Katie's mom watching them from the porch, but she'd only smiled and waved and let them enjoy the fresh air. Just the two of them.

Today they'd agreed to meet at ten o'clock, which would give Ana plenty of time to get her chores done for Babushka. Ana put on her warmest sweats and two pairs of socks. She pulled her hair into a ponytail, smashed the ponytail under a beanie, and headed to check on Mikey.

But first, Ana stopped at her mom's room and stepped past the door that was nearly always open now.

"Good morning," said her mom, already showered and dressed. "Happy New Year."

"Happy New Year." Ana picked up the family picture in the falling-apart frame. "I can't believe you kept this on your nightstand," she said. "It's awful."

Her mom laughed. "You made it. How could I not love it?" She leaned against the wall to slip her shoes on. "Hey, your dad called."

Ana examined her dad in the picture and remembered the way he'd looked at the game. For the last nine days, there had been a new version of her dad. One who actually did call and had already sent them tickets to the next Bruins–Red Wings game.

"Okay," Ana said. Even if she wasn't sure it would last and it wasn't how she'd pictured it, for now, they did seem to be moving toward okay. "I'll call him later."

Her mom grabbed her keys from the nightstand.

"You're going to work on New Year's?" Ana asked. Her mom had started going into the office a couple of hours a day for the last week.

"No," she said. "But I am going out in a bit. You'll have to ask Babushka where."

"Will you be back this afternoon?" she asked. "We need you to skate with us!"

Ana's mom smiled. "Yes, and yes. I'd love to. We can have hot chocolate and the rest of that challah when we come back inside." The ladies from the synagogue had been bringing over foil-wrapped dinners every night since the accident. Every time she opened the door for them, Ana's mom had seemed to shed the gray, sad skin she'd been wearing the last few months a little more. Now that she was almost back to normal, Ana realized how big the change had been.

"Tell Mikey I'll grab more comic books when I go out," her mom said as Ana knocked on his door.

Mikey had been a little groggy the first day after his surgery, and a little grouchy the second and third, but now that nine days had passed, he was headed back to being the smiley kid he'd been last summer.

"Hey, buddy!" Ana said. "Welcome to three hundred sixty-five days of possibility! And look," she told him as she opened his blinds. "It's a perfect day to go to the pond."

Mikey winced as he sat up a little straighter. "I thought I couldn't skate for three more weeks."

The old Ana might have ignored the doctor's orders, but she was smarter now. "I didn't say 'skate.' I said 'go to the pond.'"

"What am I going to do at the pond?"

"Oh, you'll see. Katie has a project for you. Start getting yourself dressed. I'll come back to help you finish up."

Ana was so focused on getting ready fast that she forgot about talking to Babushka until she heard her voice.

"Anastasia Ilyinichna Petrova," she called, and now Ana liked the sound of it. Babushka beckoned her in. "You will carry this suitcase downstairs."

Ana looked at the suitcase, then glanced around at Babushka's room. Babushka had kept the place spotless the whole time she'd been there, but now it was just bare. There was no little bottle of hand cream on the nightstand. No scratchy sweaters hanging in the closet. No shoes lined up neatly under the bed. (Although that last one had probably been thanks to Mikey, most of the time.)

"You're leaving?" Ana didn't move to take the suitcase. She didn't move at all.

"You said I may stay until New Year, no longer," said Babushka. "And New Year is not so expensive for flying."

"Maybe I was wrong," Ana said. She still didn't take the suitcase.

"My life is in my home, your life is here. But I will always come back if you need me. If you invite me, perhaps I will come sooner."

Ana tried to pretend the answer was good enough, but it wasn't.

Babushka could tell. "Come in," she said. "Sit down. We talk."

But when they were actually sitting there, facing each other on the stiff, stripped mattress, it was hard to think of the right thing to say. Finally, Ana started.

"Why did you come here?"

"Because Thanksgiving is about family, and Hanukkah is about rebuilding," Babushka reminded Ana. "I thought I must rebuild your family myself. Foolish old woman."

Ana hadn't disagreed with Babushka for a while, but she knew she needed to on this one. "You did rebuild us. Or at least, you got us off to a good start."

Babushka frowned and shook her head. "In my life, I have one job to do: raise a good son. Instead, I raise a son who left his family." Her shoulders dropped. "This is my fault. This is my job to fix."

"It's not," Ana said. "I thought it was my job, and Mikey thought it was his, and you thought it was yours. My mom thought it was hers too, I think, and it crushed her. But he was the one just standing there in the arena, not even taking off his dumb skates."

"He was a good boy." Babushka looked up at Ana, like she was asking her to believe.

Ana thought about that. Her dad had been to lots of her hockey games. He'd taken her out for waffle fries after wins sometimes, and shown her little videos he'd taken of stuff she could work on. And stuff that had made him proud.

"He was a pretty good dad too, for a long time. He told me a lot of your stories when I was little, like about that girl with the doll."

Babushka's eyes lit up. "Ah, yes! Vasilisa! Did you read the ending?"

Ana shook her head. She'd totally forgotten. "Was her family ever the same again? Did her parents magically come back?"

Babushka shook her head and made a small, clucking sound. "No, child."

"But she was okay anyway, right?"

"Yes."

Ana's mouth snuck into a smile. "And she survived the witch?"

Babushka cackled. "She did. And the witch survived her." She pushed herself up from the bed with a sigh. "No more time for chitchat. Bring that downstairs," she commanded.

Ana struggled with the weight of the suitcase all the way downstairs and out the door, but her mom took it from her in the driveway. "Thank you," she said. "Will you go get your brother?"

Mikey could walk okay now, but he let Ana piggyback

him down the stairs. She covered him in layers of warm, waterproof clothes and led him to the front door.

"Wait a second," Mikey said. "I thought we were going to the pond."

"We have to say good-bye to Babushka first."

Mikey frowned. "Really?" He studied Ana's face. "Am I supposed to be happy?"

Ana shook her head. "You're supposed to feel however you feel. It's okay if you're sad. It's okay if you'll miss her."

"Is it okay if I like her cooking now?" he asked.

Ana thought about that one. "It has to be, because I kind of like it too."

Babushka waited for them in the driveway. She reached into her handbag and took out the pocket watch.

"For you," she said to Ana. "I am sorry I said you stole it. It was always for you."

"It's okay," said Ana, holding the watch close to her heart. "And thank you."

Babushka reached into her bag again. This time, she held a little dreidel. It had been so long since they'd done anything but light the candles that Ana had almost forgotten about that part of Hanukkah.

"For you," she said to Mikey.

Mikey stared down at the toy. "Hanukkah is over."

Babushka grunted. "I do not give Hanukkah presents. This is New Year present."

Mikey tried to spin the top on his palm. "I don't even know how to play."

"I do," Ana said. "I can teach you."

Babushka showed Mikey the Hebrew letters on the sides of the little top. "Do you know what these letters stand for?" she asked.

Mikey shrugged. "Happy Hanukkah?"

Babushka shook her head. "Nes gadol haya sham." She touched one side as she said each word. "That means, 'A great miracle happened here.'"

Mikey's eyes lit up. "Is it me?" he asked. "Am I the miracle?"

"We give dreidels to children," Babushka said, "because each child is a miracle." She put one arm around Mikey's shoulders and the other around Ana's. "But especially my grandchildren." Then she blustered away, muttering about the dirty Boston air getting something in her eyes.

Ana stood behind Mikey and hugged across his shoulders, pulling him close enough that she could smell his coconut shampoo. She heard the sniffle first as they watched the car disappear around the corner, then felt the drop of a tear in the gap between her coat and her mittens.

Okay, Mikey hadn't even made it ten hours into the New Year without crying, but Ana couldn't blame him. She might have been crying a little herself. Maybe.

Ana cleared her throat. "Are you ready to go to the pond?"

"I haven't even had breakfast!" Mikey protested.

"I know," said Ana. "That's part of the surprise."

Ana piled Mikey on the sled, then ran back to the fridge. There, on the bottom shelf, was a half-moon of candy bar pie.

Mrs. Burton had come over the night before and taught Ana's mom how to make it. Ana had been pretty surprised to see her mom baking, and even more surprised that it had turned out perfectly. But the most surprising thing of all was *why* Mrs. Burton said she'd come.

"Because your Babushka taught me so much. What a wonderful person."

Ana didn't even argue.

When they got to the pond, Mikey started stuffing his face with candy bar pie. It only took a few minutes before Katie stepped out of her back door.

"There she is," Mikey said. "Your pair." He sighed. "I sure wish mine hadn't moved to Detroit."

Ana wrinkled her nose. "You think Dad's your pair?"

Mikey shrugged. "Maybe."

"Oh, buddy. That's like pairing a chocolate chip with a glop of mud."

Mikey laughed. "So who's my pair?"

Ana reached over and swiped some whipped cream with her finger. As it melted on her tongue, she thought about Mikey's question.

"I don't think it's about pairs. Pairs are good, but you need more than two. You need a whole family."

Mikey crushed a crumb in the bottom of the pie tin. "We don't have that anymore either."

"Of course we do! Whole doesn't mean two or four, and it's not just the people who live in your house." Katie's parents appeared on the porch, and Ana thought she saw the glint of skates in their hands too. "It's like your paper chain, maybe. Except it's going in all directions, and growing all the time."

"But those can break," Mikey said.

Ana wished he wasn't right about that. "Yeah, they can. You have to protect them. But they can be fixed too.

You can make them stronger."

"Happy New Year!" Katie's dad called as he approached the pond. "We've missed you two at our house. Mrs. Burton keeps buying food, and when I go to the pantry, it's still there!"

"We'll fix that," Ana said. "But let me work up an appetite first."

Katie sat next to Mikey and handed him a little bag of red paper strips. "A new chain for Valentine's Day," she said. "If you pinch the top like this, and the bottom like that, and put another little dot of glue right there, they're hearts!"

Mikey started folding and gluing right away.

Ana and Katie skated the rest of the morning, and Ana couldn't believe how much longer Katie could go already before she got out of breath. Gradually, the rest of the neighborhood kids joined them.

Ana had worried that Mikey would get bored or cold and want to go back to bed. But every time she looked over, his chain had grown a little longer, and somebody new was there to talk to him. First Katie's dad, showing him how to make tiny snowmen from his spot on the sled. Then Katie's mom, sneaking him a cookie from her coat pocket. Even Jarek—Ana watched that one closely, but he was only there for a few seconds. Long enough to say sorry, Ana suspected.

Ana tipped her face to the sun and counted all the planes, their trails crisscrossing the sky. Maybe Babushka was in one of them; maybe she was looking down right now.

"Thank you," Ana whispered, just in case.

"Thank you," she whispered again, to Mikey and Katie and her mom and even her dad, to the Burtons and her hockey friends and all the people who had been like family to her, who had caught her and lifted her and made her life better.

Katie came up and handed Ana a hockey stick. "Thank *you*," Katie said.

Ana dropped the old puck she'd taken from under her mattress. She tapped it with one side of her stick, then the other, just getting the feel of it back into her fingers as Katie got into position for another non-contact hockey lesson.

Then, from across the pond, Ana heard the sound of Mikey's laugh. She looked over to see her mom pulling him onto her lap, teasing and trying to steal the very last of the candy bar pie.

He was going to be okay. And so was her mom, and Katie. So was she, really.

They were all going to be okay.

A great miracle happened here.

Author's Note

THE VERY FIRST seeds of this story came from a book my grandmother read to me when I was young: *The Snow Child* by Freya Littledale. I was lucky to have parents, grandparents, teachers, and librarians who surrounded me with stories as I was growing up, and those stories became part of me. It was that idea of a broad mix of stories shaping each of us—with *The Snow Child* at its center—that became the heart of this book.

It takes a leap of faith and a lot of research to write about cultures and experiences beyond one's own, and I'm grateful for the chance to do so. I grew up hearing stories of my own ancestors and feeling part of a larger family and heritage. However, one quarter of my own ancestry is Eastern European, and it is those ancestors my family has always known the least about, in spite of my aunt's years of searching. This book is primarily an attempt to tell a story that spoke to me—but in a small way, I think it's also an attempt to make a connection with a part of myself I still know very little about.

As I drafted this book, two groups came to my hometown and brought pieces of Russia with them: the Moscow Ballet and Nikolai Massenkoff & the Russian Folk Festival. It was such an honor to be immersed in their stories, told through music and dance and spoken words.

Throughout the writing process, I was fortunate to have the cultural, religious, and even medical expertise of so many friends and expert readers, who are listed in the acknowledgments. Any mistakes are my own.

Finally, I turned to many resources, both in print and online as I tried to get this one just right. Here are a few books that I found particularly helpful.

Russian Fairy Tales by Aleksandr Afanasev, Alexander Alexeieff, Norbert Guterman, Roman Jakobson

Natasha's Dance: A Cultural History of Russia by Orlando Figes

Living Judaism by Wayne D. Dosick

All About Hanukkah by Madeline Wikler and Judyth Groner

Twenty Things Adoptive Kids Wish Their Adoptive Parents Knew by Sherrie Eldridge

How It Feels to Be Adopted by Jill Krementz

Acknowledgments

THIS BOOK IS dedicated to my family, and I mean that by every possible definition of the word.

Thank you to Lucy, Halle, Jack, and Robbie. It's my greatest joy to fall asleep and wake up under the same roof with you, and to spend so many happy hours together in between.

Thank you to my parents and siblings and nieces and nephews of both the Braithwaite and Vickers varieties.

What a lucky thing to have you all in my life and to so fully be a part of two incredible families.

Thanks to my writing family: Helen Boswell, Tasha Seegmiller, Rosalyn Eves, and especially Erin Shakespear, who joined me on a journey to Boston to research this book and made the whole thing absolutely delightful.

Thanks to the eclectic family of helpers who loaned their expertise in all sorts of things so I could get this right: Ann Braden, Jeannie Mobley, Jennifer Stewart, Chris Hayes, Elly Swartz, Jed Montgomery, Franny Ilany, Gia Miller, Jenny Call, Elsie Call, Ryan Decker, Alice Crandall, Ariana Fuller, Hannah Olsen, and Anastasia Randall. Any mistakes are my own.

Thanks to my publishing family: Emilia Rhodes for bringing out the best in this story, and Ammi-Joan Paquette for making me believe I can write any of the stories in my heart. Thank you to Jen Klonsky, Alice Jerman, Maya Myers, Alison Klapthor, Jessica Berg, Gina Rizzo, Molly Motch, Megan Barlog, and the entire team at Harper. A huge and heartfelt thank you to Sara Not for creating the most beautiful book covers I've ever seen.

Finally, thank you to all the readers. I'm claiming you as family too.

Don't miss *Like Magic* by
ELAINE VICKERS

"Readers will imagine themselves right smack in the middle of this book—solving mysteries, making connections, and creating beauty alongside Malia, Jada, and Grace."

–Liz Garton Scanlon, author of *The Great Good Summer*